THE MIDWINTER WATCH

John Gordon, a Geordie by birth, moved to East Anglia with his family at the age of twelve. He served in the Navy during the Second World War and afterwards worked as a journalist. He is widely recognised as one of the finest contemporary writers of horror and the supernatural for young people. His books include *The Giant Under the Snow*, *The House on the Brink*, *The Burning Baby and Other Ghosts*, *Gilray's Ghost* and *The Flesh Eater*. Married with two grown-up children, he lives in Norwich.

Books by the same author

THE MIDWINTER WATCH

JOHN GORDON

WALKER BOOKS
AND SUBSIDIARIES
LONDON · BOSTON · SYDNEY

For Nisha and Dileep

First published 1998 by Walker Books Ltd
87 Vauxhall Walk, London SE11 5HJ

This edition published 1999

2 4 6 8 10 9 7 5 3

Text © 1998 John Gordon
Cover illustration © 1998 Paul Robinson

This book has been typeset in Sabon.

Printed in Great Britain by Cox & Wyman Ltd
Reading, Berkshire

The right of John Gordon to be identified as author
of this work has been asserted by him in accordance with the
Copyright, Designs and Patents Act 1988.

British Library Cataloguing in Publication Data
A catalogue record for this book is available
from the British Library.

ISBN 0-7445-6959-1

CONTENTS

THE SNOW TRAIN

Snow. Sophie stood on the hillside and looked out over the valley. The village below seemed to have snuggled down into white bedclothes so soft and deep that it was in no hurry to arouse itself. The hills in the distance had hunched their shoulders to bear the weight of the most recent blizzard, and their smoothness was as perfect as the silence that lay over the whole landscape.

"Everything's different," she said, and wished it was.

Jack watched her breath hang in the air before it vanished. He breathed the same air, but suddenly it looked different coming from a girl's mouth. Or so he thought, and then tried to unthink it. He knew she was sad, but he didn't want to say so. "Are you cold?" he asked.

"How can anyone be cold in snow like

this?" she said.

For more than a week the snow had closed in on Lott's Bend, and for the last three days the village had been cut off. It had never happened before and she should have enjoyed it – would have enjoyed it if everything had been as it once was. But it wasn't.

Jack looked back down the slope. They were out of breath but they had not come far. The lane was choked between its banks so they had been forced to climb out and continue through the fields, but it had been heavy going and even now they were barely higher than the rooftops below, and the sledge they were tugging was often bogged down. He laughed and shouted, "Sophie's right – everything's different!" Snow as deep as this was what he had always wanted at Christmas.

Simon, in his usual way, brought them down to earth. "It's only snow," he said. "White rain. Everything's the same underneath."

"That's the trouble," said Sophie without thinking.

Jack knew what she meant. Sophie was not happy where she lived, and it was because of the snow. It had forced her and her mother to leave their own home. "Christmas in two days," he said but, for once, this did not make her smile. He saw what was on her mind but he couldn't think of anything to say so he made as if to push Simon into a snowdrift, then changed his mind and pushed Sophie instead. She was nicer to handle, much softer. She squealed and fought back and was suddenly herself again, fighting him, pink cheeked and laughing.

But Simon had remained motionless, staring into the distance. "That's strange," he said.

They drew apart, gasping and shaking snow from their heads and shoulders as they looked in the same direction, away from the edge of the huddled rooftops below. The trees wore white wigs and the hedges were all but submerged in the new landscape, but there was nothing unexpected.

"I don't see anything strange," said Jack.

"There." Simon, calm as always, nodded to where the houses ended and the hills began to climb. "I saw something in the cutting."

The railway cutting. None of them could remember as far back as the time when trains wound their way through the hills bringing passengers to the tiny railway station at the end of Station Lane. The old wooden waiting room and ticket office now stood empty, and the cutting that took the line through the slopes was overgrown. Nothing moved, and Sophie said so.

Simon ignored her. "There it is again," he said.

Trees had grown haphazardly along the

sides of the disused railway, and their humped shapes, white on white, showed them where it was beneath the snow.

"There's still nothing," said Jack.

Which pleased Simon. "You're looking straight at it," he said smugly.

And still all they could see were the cauliflower humps of trees. But then one of the trees dissolved, only to grow again just as suddenly.

"White smoke!" cried Sophie. "Someone's burning something in the cutting."

"I know what it is!" Jack had made his mind up. "Someone has been cut off by the snow and is sending up a smoke signal! We've got to dig our way through." He was already heading downhill.

Simon smiled at Sophie. "Jack the Giantkiller's at it again," he said.

"I'm going with him."

"You'll only be embarrassed. It's just someone with a bonfire."

But Sophie didn't care. Simon always thought he knew best. Maybe he did, but she'd rather be wrong with Jack than stand aloof with Simon. Jack was an embarrassment often enough, always blurting out the first crazy thing that came into his head; but pale, tall Simon with his straw hair only made her feel small. His intelligence scared her a bit, which was what he intended.

10

The going was easier when they reached the village street. Snow was piled up on both sides to make space for traffic, but there were no black tyre marks for there was nowhere for cars to go and even the ruts made by tractors as they headed out to battle with the drifts had been covered by new snow.

It was very quiet, and the silence deepened as they turned into Station Lane. Jack looked up at the sky. The bright morning had darkened as the clouds trundled over the hills loaded with more snow. It was what he wanted. At this rate they would still be cut off over Christmas in spite of the tractors, and his mind filled with impossible things ... such as seeing reindeer hoofprints across rooftops on Christmas morning. Long ago he had believed such things, and now he was making a fool of himself about smoke signals, so he made a game of it, galloping ahead with the toboggan shouting, "No time to lose!"

"What if it's only a train?" said Sophie. "Perhaps they sent it through on the old line – with a snowplough or something."

Simon was greatly amused. "Only you would think of something as ridiculous as that, Sophie. They took the track up years ago."

"All right, teacher!" She put out her tongue.

"Childish." He raised his eyes to the sky. "Both of you."

Jack slowed down and turned around to see her grimace at Simon. She was even pretty when she was making herself ugly. He didn't understand it, but he wasn't worried. You didn't have to understand everything, especially not miracles ... so maybe the track was still there under the weeds that choked the cutting. But the rest of what she had said could not be right. "It can't be a train," he said, "because all that smoke would mean it's a steam train, and there aren't any of them left. Sorry, Sophie."

She drew in her breath. The boys knew. They always knew – or thought they did. But she knew what she'd seen and she wasn't going to let them stop her. She tugged the toboggan from Jack's hand and ploughed ahead.

There were no houses in Station Lane and it stretched ahead of them covered in unbroken snow. No one had come this way since the snows began, but as they turned into it a pair of hidden eyes was watching.

Sophie plunged on. "It's not all that deep," she panted. The lane ran through a long avenue of trees which had given it some shelter.

"Deep enough." Jack ignored Simon's sensible plea to leave the sledge behind and he helped Sophie to lug it along.

At the far end of the lane, in the cold gloom of the station ticket office, a man stood watching them. He wore dark clothes which blended with the dark shadows, and he hummed to himself, trying to keep his temper under control as he watched the three figures floundering towards the station. But his anger burst through.

"Damn the snow! Damn those kids! Where has that damned man got to!"

His nostrils narrowed as he drew in his breath and regained control of himself. "Vexatious." His thin lips brought an extra hiss to the word. "Extremely vexatious. But no harm done." The lips vanished among the wrinkles in his narrow face as he smiled to himself. "No harm, not yet, but damn the man!"

He had time to look around. He went to the bleak iron fireplace. No fire had burned there for many winters but an old black kettle still stood on the hob. He took off his glove and stooped to touch it as if expecting it to be warm, and when he found it was icy he hummed to himself, thinking. "Oddity upon oddity," he murmured. "I anticipated a warmer welcome than this from friend Reginald. What the devil is the fool up to? The pub, is it? Swilling, is he?"

Suddenly he broke off and lifted his head, listening.

They had paused for breath at the edge of the station yard. It had never been a big yard but now it was even smaller, a dish of whiteness where the wind had swirled snow into the bushes that surrounded it. They stood and listened. Nothing but the silence of the snow … except that, from beyond the station building, there came the sound of the gentle hiss of steam and, even quieter, the rhythmical breathing of an engine.

Simon heard it but was never going to let Sophie get the better of him. "No passengers," he said. "It's a goods train loaded with food and stuff for the shop, and maybe some mail … all those Christmas cards you didn't get, Sophie."

It would have been pleasant to strangle him, she thought, but Jack distracted her. He was pointing to the station buildings. They hid the engine, but near the middle there was a gap that led to the platform. Through it she caught a glimpse of a railway carriage.

The man in the ticket office moved quickly. He glanced to the door and then back to the fireplace. On the wall above the mantelpiece was the old railway clock that had not been wound up in years. He looked at it and then, ridiculously, checked the time against a carriage clock he carried in a small wooden box as he hissed under his breath, "Pub, is it! Beer, is it! Time is running out for you, Reg Boston!"

He had locked the clock and its box into a suitcase when he heard them kicking into the snowdrift that covered the three steps up to the station. He stood motionless, listening, as Jack, who was in the lead, slipped and fell.

The whistle and the chuff of steam came together as Jack picked himself up, and their feet thudded on the bare boards as they ran past the ticket office on to the platform. The last carriage and the guard's van were already sliding by, and the rumble of wheels died swiftly away as a spiral of snow whipped up from the drifts closed in and hid the rear of the speeding train. Then it was gone as if it had never been there. They were alone. No one left and no one came on the bare platform.

"It was just as I expected," said Simon, taking over Sophie's idea. "They've sent a snowplough through to clear the track."

But Sophie was not listening. She had turned her head, and Jack saw such alarm dart into her face that he spun around.

A man stood outside the ticket office. They must have run past him without seeing, and now he blocked the passage back to the open yard. He wore a long black overcoat and he was not tall, but he confronted them like a warrior guarding a pass, and for an instant they thought he was about to advance on them from the shadows. But then he spoke.

"Good morning," he said. He wore black gloves and he raised his black hat by just a fraction, which had the effect of putting more

15

of his face in shadow. He was old. His mouth had a bleak look to it, and the skin of his face was wrinkled and the colour of mushrooms.

They murmured a reply, but none of them made an effort to go forward.

"There is no need to be afraid." The stranger seemed amused. "I do not eat young persons." His thin lips curved upwards as sharp as a sickle. "I carve them on Christmas day, and devour them slice by slice."

THE TEN BOB NOTE

"Carved into slices!" Laughter grated in the stranger's throat. "Just my little joke."

None of them took the trouble to laugh. "Were you on the train?" Jack asked.

The thin lips were suddenly pinched in and the voice chopped like an axe. "What train!"

Instantly Jack swung back at him. "You know what train I mean!"

Trouble. Jack's temper had flashed. Sophie wanted to shut her eyes on it, but she kept them steadily on the stranger.

There was a long pause before the lips curved again and what had started as a venomous hiss became a chuckle. "If only there had been a train, there would have been a taxi here to meet me." The stranger smiled, looking at each of them in turn. "Is it much further to the village? Is there an inn?"

Simon, not trusting Jack's temper, said,

"We were sure we saw a train. There was steam…"

"Blown snow," said the man.

"A definite rumble…"

"Snow sliding on the slope."

"Carriages going by…"

"The wind came swirling past the station just a moment ago."

"But we saw…"

"Nothing… The blizzard dazzles the eyes and upsets the brain. I seemed to see many peculiar things on my way here." The stranger spread his hands as if he were helpless. "Wherever this is."

He was surprised when they told him. "But that is miles out of my way! My car was overtaken by the storm and I got lost in the hills." He waved a hand. "The car is still out there somewhere, and how I got here on foot I hardly know." He caught Jack's eye examining him for traces of his journey. "And I have been brushing myself down in that ticket office ever since. Now I need to find an inn – if there is an inn, is there?"

"The Blacksmith's Arms," said Jack. He lived next door.

"Then direct me to it." The stranger picked up his suitcase, turned sharply and marched to the snow-covered steps, where he stumbled and almost fell. It affected his dignity and he stood up to his knees in a drift, savage with himself and everyone else. "Damn and blast this filthy weather!"

And Jack relented a fraction. He pulled the toboggan closer. "We can carry your bag if you like," he said.

"Keen to earn a few bob, are you?" The words were spat out.

Jack reddened. "That's not what I meant!"

Their eyes locked, and the stranger suddenly thrust his case towards Jack's stomach. "Put it on your sledge," he snapped.

Not Jack. He stood still.

"Take it!"

Sophie watched. Jack was never going to move. Wasn't there enough trouble without this?

"Jack." She found herself moving forward. "Let's help him. Don't forget his car got stuck in the snow ... he's had a long walk."

She was the only one Jack would have obeyed at that moment. He took the bag. "But I don't want paying," he said.

The stranger had nothing more to say, and they trudged in silence to the village street. The few people who were out and about, mostly clearing paths in front of their houses, spoke to them as they passed and plainly wanted to talk to the stranger, but he paused for nothing.

At the Blacksmith's Arms it was Simon he trusted to carry the bag inside for him. They saw him thrust something into Simon's hand

and then abruptly turn away.

"He's not so bad after all." Simon opened his hand to show them what he had been given. "He told me to share it."

But there was something wrong. The bank-note was a strange colour; it was rust red, and when they looked closer they saw that its value was not given in pounds but in shillings.

"Shillings!" Simon was disgusted. "Ten shillings! That's old money, isn't it? I'm going to take it back."

It was Sophie who persuaded him not to confront the stranger again. Jack merely shrugged. The stranger could keep his money.

Simon's father laughed when he saw the ten shilling note. "These things haven't been around for over thirty years," he said. "He must have seen you coming, old son, and offloaded his old currency. That'll teach you to rely on paper money."

Another lecture coming up, thought Simon. That was the trouble with a father who taught such things at the university in the city. But his mother caught sight of the note and was charmed by it.

"Ten bob!" she cried. "It's years since I've seen one of those. Isn't it lovely!"

Simon sighed. A mother who taught even-ing classes in creative writing would go on about what things looked like when what

20

he really wanted to know was how much it was worth.

"Face value?" his father mused. "Fifty pence. And only slightly more if you took it to a dealer. You can't actually spend it any longer."

"Thanks a bundle." Simon was despondent, and his mother noticed.

"Oh, just look at his poor little face!" She pouted and made comforting kissing noises at him. "And just before Christmas, too." She was prone to tease him when she felt happy, and she was always happy when the tree in the parlour was decorated and she was making Christmas puddings, as now.

"Give me a break," said Simon.

His father, as tall and lanky as Simon had worked out that he himself would one day become, stooped to pull aside the curtain at the kitchen window and look up at the hills. "Still blowing a blizzard at the top of Scaly-bank," he said. "Not a chance of getting through today." He sighed, because he played squash at the university courts and today was to have been Christmas drinks time with his mates, but that was in the city and far out of reach.

Simon opened his mouth to tell him he could have taken a train if he'd been out and about a bit earlier, but thought better of it.

"That friend of yours who gave you the

duff note was lucky to make it on foot," said his father.

Simon had already given the stranger's account of the car caught in the snow drift and the path he'd found along the cutting, but nothing would make him mention the train. It was far too much like believing in a dream.

"I'm going to frame it," said his mother, and made him put the little russet coloured oblong on the mantelpiece. "So I'll buy it from you." She wiped her hands and took a five pound note from her purse. "As it's Christmas."

"Good rate of exchange," said his father. "It'll make you popular with the others. Here's a quid to help you split it three ways."

"Why can't you two be like this all the year round?" said Simon, and had to flee the kitchen.

Jack's home was the old forge next to the Blacksmith's Arms. The forge was now a garage, and his father had a car up on the ramps and was working beneath it when Jack told him about the train.

"Boy," said his father, who did not seem to have heard, "the two coldest jobs in the world are a shepherd at lambing time and workin' in a garage. Shut that door."

Jack's father was a Smith from a long line of Smiths who had run the blacksmith's shop in the village and lived in Old Forge Cottage that joined the smithy. He still called the garage the smithy because it had changed very little over the years, and Jack himself was prone to leave the door open as if the forge in the corner was still stacked with coal – "just like all you Smiths" his mother said – but he closed it now as snowflakes came feathering in.

"But it's true, Dad," he said. "We saw it, Simon and me." He did not mention Sophie. He'd got into the habit of being quiet about her, ever since he'd noticed how pretty she was. People got ideas.

"Just look at the state of that." Mr Smith hauled a rusting brake pipe from underneath the car. "Saw what?" he asked his son.

"The train."

"Oh-ah." His father nodded, still looking at the brake pipe. "He'd have lost them brakes on a hill as like as not ... and that would've put the lights out on someone's Christmas tree. Not that anyone's goin' anywhere in this weather."

"The train did," said Jack. "It came into the station just now – the station up the road," he added in case his father thought it happened somewhere else. "Must've had a snow plough on the front." He hesitated. "Although I didn't see it."

His father was a square sort of man, not very tall, and he stood squarely facing his son, his hands black with grease and his overalls showing more and more grease downwards from the waist until at his ankles it was impossible to tell where the blackness of his overall legs became the sooty black of his garageman's boots. But his eyes were bright blue and sharp.

"There ain't been a train through here since they closed the line – before you was born. They even took the rails up, if you remember."

"No, I don't remember, do I? But they couldn't have, because I saw it! And a man got off. Well, he said he didn't, but I reckon he must have because the snow's too deep to walk through."

"You ain't having me on, are you, Jack?" The most usual expression on his father's face was a slight smile, and it was there now.

"It's true, Dad. I saw it. And there was this man. We carried his bag and he gave us some money, only –"

He broke off because his father's smile diminished just a shade. He did not like his son accepting money for doing someone a good turn. "Only what?" he asked.

"Only it wasn't hardly a tip at all. He gave us half a quid in old money, so we can't spend it."

Mr Smith's smile broadened. "Then you was done, wasn't you?" He didn't say serve you right, which Jack was thankful for. In fact, his father let him off the hook. "It were blowing a blizzard when you was up at the old

24

station, was it? I expect it blew snow in your eyes and swirled it up a bit till you thought you saw something that weren't properly there at all. Such things happen, specially when you want them to." He was rubbing grease remover on his hands. "Tell you what I'll do, though. I'm goin' over to the Blacksmith's in a minute" – which was something every Smith had done every lunchtime for a hundred years – "and I'll keep my eyes open for that rum shoot you tell me about. And if I see him I'll ask him how he managed to get through all this blasted snow."

Sophie was struggling through snow up to her knees before she realized she had gone past her home. Not that she called it home – not now or ever. It was Mr Boston's home, and she hated him.

She looked ahead. Her true home, where she and her mother had lived until a few days ago, was still out of sight where the road bent around the long wall that surrounded Heron Hall, and she could not get to it. If her father had been alive there would have been a curl of blue woodsmoke above the flank of the hill, and in a few minutes she would have been sitting in the chimney corner warming her toes while he brought in the Christmas logs. But not now. He had been dead two years.

Sophie had long ago learned not to cry when

she thought of him, so it was the cold that made her wipe her eyes with the cuff of her glove as she turned back. Ivy, like a winter nightcap, hung over the wall around the grounds of Heron Hall, and she trudged back to where the tall iron gates were wedged open by the snow cleared from the drive. Just inside, the gatehouse made a Christmas card against the trees, but she kept her head down so as not to look at it and like it. It was Reg Boston's house, and she was forced to live there.

His pick-up truck was not in the yard, and as she kicked off her boots in the back porch she called out, "Where is he?"

"Reg is up at the Hall, Sophie." Her mother was laying a table, very slowly, fork by fork. "He's helping Toby Heron."

"Clearing snow, I expect."

"I really couldn't say." Lucy Nelson had not always been so vague. It had crept over her since her husband died. It frightened Sophie, and irritated her. She frowned as her mother drifted around the table yet again, needlessly adjusting the cutlery. "Is he is having his lunch there?" she asked.

Her mother looked at her as if she had not heard.

"Is he having his lunch with Toby?" Sophie repeated. "Because I hope he is."

"Sophie," her mother's head drooped, "I wish you wouldn't say things like that." That's how it always was whenever Sophie said even one word against Reg Boston. "You used to like him when Dad was alive."

Things were different then. Reg Boston, the big man who lived in the gatehouse, Toby Heron's friend, used to visit them often with Toby. She remembered how he would toss her in the air when she was small and make her laugh, but how sometimes he would throw her so high she was afraid and she would wriggle free from the large hands that lifted her too easily. Everyone said Reg Boston was a man who had fallen on hard times, and he was lucky to have known Toby Heron since they were boys together because Toby had given him a place to live for as long as he needed it. In return Reg Boston was to help Toby with all the work that was needed on Heron Hall, because the house, as Toby himself told everyone, would soon be falling apart for want of money. But Boston went away for long periods, and Sophie had heard her father say one day that he very much doubted whether he earned his keep, and her mother had smiled and said, "Poor Toby is far too soft-hearted."

But when Sophie's father died, Reg Boston suddenly took it upon himself to help them in every way he could. Lucy Nelson had come to rely on him.

"So why are you behaving like this,

Sophie?" It was almost as if her mother had been reading her thoughts. "Reg is a friend of ours."

"Of yours, you mean. Why did you let him take us away from home when the snow came?"

"You very well know it was getting impossible for us to stay there. Reg was very kind to take us in; he rescued us."

"Dad wouldn't have let him."

"Oh, Sophie, not that again!"

Sophie watched her. A helpless sadness seemed to be always on her mother's face, so that even her prettiness had begun to fade. And Sophie could not bring herself to tell her of the expression she had seen on Reg Boston's face as he had insisted on hurrying them out of their house and into his own. He had looked into far too many rooms to see what they had, and Sophie had pushed open a door to see him going through the drawers of her father's desk. She had startled him, and the greed she had seen swimming in his handsome dark eyes had turned instantly to anger. He had slammed the drawers shut and locked the desk. "Tell your mother," he said, "that I'm making sure we leave nothing valuable lying about," and he put the key in his pocket. From that moment he and Sophie had not trusted each other.

Now she watched her mother's vague fingers touch a spoon to move it a useless fraction of an inch, and she could stand it no longer.

"Mum!" she cried. "Don't!" And she lunged forward and pressed her mother's hand to the table.

Lucy Nelson was startled. "What is it, Sophie?"

"I don't want to stay here! We could get back up the lane if we tried."

"Reg has told me we can't."

"We don't have to believe him!"

"But it's so good of him to take us in, Sophie. We would hurt his feelings if we ran away now."

"I don't care! I don't like him!"

"Why not, my pet?" It was a long time since she had held Sophie by both hands, but she did so now. "You don't understand what a big sacrifice he is making for us."

"He's not making a sacrifice – he's doing it for himself. He wants to marry you!" The words had leapt out even before the thought was in her mind. She gazed, horrified, into her mother's face.

A faint pinkness came into Lucy Nelson's cheeks. "What a silly idea," she said, but her voice was too calm. In that moment Sophie knew she had thought about it. "You can't!" she cried.

Her mother said nothing, and Sophie dragged her hands free just as tyres crunched

29

the snow somewhere outside. Reg Boston was coming back, and she could not face him. She jammed on her boots and ran out headlong, looking along the drive towards the Hall, and missed seeing the squat little car that had turned in through the gates. It was her own dash that sent her into the car's front wing. It had stopped before she hit it, but she fell back and was still sprawling when the driver got out and crouched beside her.

"Sophie!" Toby Heron's round face was full of anxiety. "Are you hurt?" And then he assumed the worst. "Where are you hurt? Tell me!"

She sat up, shaking her head. He took a deep breath and blew out his cheeks, stuttering slightly as he blamed himself. "You," he said. "I mean me. I didn't expect to see you. It's all my fault. I'd forgotten you'd come to live down here at the gatehouse and I just turned in through the gate in the normal way – and there ... and there you were."

"But I'm all right, Mr Heron." After all that had happened it felt unnatural to call him by his first name. He did not seem to notice.

"But you're very pale, Sophie." He helped her to her feet. "Let me take you in to your mother."

She resisted. "I don't want to go in."

"Sophie?" He realized something was wrong.

"I just don't want to go back in there." His eyes still questioned her. She hung her head and muttered, "I want to go back home."

He stood there, with a sprinkle of snow on his bulky overcoat and squashed porkpie hat, worried about her, and as helpless and plump as a snowman. But he had guessed something of what was on her mind. "Cheer up, Sophie, Christmas will soon be over." He meant it as a joke, but it didn't work. "I know," he said more seriously, "Reg Boston is a fearsome great brute, but he's a good sort. He got you here when the snows came, before I had the chance to offer. I'm sure he's made you very comfortable."

But he's your friend and you never say anything bad about anybody, she thought. So how can I tell you I hate him?

"You've got something on your mind, Sophie."

"No," she said, and then in desperation to stop him asking more questions, blurted out the first thing that came into her mind. "It's just that I can't understand how that train got through this morning."

It was a very stupid thing to say and she saw the bewilderment in his face. At any minute he would think that the bump had affected her.

"A train with a snowplough came into the station this morning," she said, "and a man got off." She looked up at him, expecting him

31

to smile, but he was waiting for her to go on. "He gave us a tip when we carried his bag on Jack's sledge, but it was very old money – a ten shilling note."

She tried to laugh at that, but his expression prevented it. He stared at her with his mouth slightly open. "Train?" he asked as though it was something he did not wish to hear. She nodded. "And just one man?"

"Yes," said Sophie.

"What did he look like?"

She told him all she knew about the stranger, but it did not seem to be enough. "And he said he came by train, did he?" Toby asked.

"No. He told us he came by car that got stuck in the snow, but –" she paused as something occurred to her, "but he didn't look as if he'd been walking through snow." She had suddenly recalled his shoes; they had been quite clean.

The sound of a motor made Toby look away towards the Hall. A pick-up truck was coming along the drive. He turned back towards Sophie. "You are sure about the train?"

She nodded.

"Who else saw it?"

"Just three of us."

He glanced away towards the pick-up. It was much closer.

"Sophie." He leant towards her, and he was

32

no longer the vague Toby that everyone knew. He spoke intensely. "I believe you, but nobody else will."

"What about the man?"

"Leave him to me." He lowered his voice because the pick-up had come up to them and the engine cut. "Say nothing about the train, and tell the others to keep it to themselves." Their eyes met. "Just between you three and me. It's vital." He turned away to smile at Reg Boston as he stepped down from the cab.

GETTING DARK

Reg Boston was strong. He was also quiet and always went about the house in his socks, which made him more silent than such a big man should be. Now, when he stood at the kitchen fire with his back towards them, he seemed more secretive than ever. He had a weightlifter's back with broad shoulders, a thick neck and a cropped head as round as a cannonball. It frightened Sophie. His heavy, handsome face never altered, but his back was hunched as though he was containing his anger.

"What were you and Toby Heron talking about outside in the snow?" he said softly without turning around.

"Nothing," said Sophie.

He was motionless except that his shirt tightened over his shoulders. "I thought I heard someone say something about a train."

Sophie looked at her mother. "I didn't say anything to you about trains, did I, Mum?"

He turned around fast enough to prevent Lucy Nelson replying, and he cut across her without raising his voice. "I didn't ask what you said to your mother. I wanted to know what was interesting enough to keep you standing outside in the snow without a coat." His large, dark eyes bulged slightly, and she stared back silently while the clock on the mantel ticked out the seconds.

It was Lucy Nelson who fidgeted, and a gleam of her old self returned as she defended her daughter. "Sophie had just gone out to fetch some logs from the woodpile," she said. "That's why she didn't have a coat."

He turned the liquid darkness of his gaze from one to the other as though he suspected they were keeping something from him, but he sat down at the table without saying more.

Mealtimes were awkward at the gatehouse, and the snow was to blame. Lucy Nelson wanted to repay Reg Boston for taking them in so she had taken over the cooking and tried to get meals to please him, but she was the sort of cook who needed trips to supermarkets, and the towns were out of reach. He never complained, but she was nervous when he soon pushed his plate away. He thanked her, as he always did. Reg Boston was a polite man. "I'm afraid I can't hang about all day, Lucy," he said. "Things to do."

"Where are you off to now?" She forced herself to smile, taking an interest, but he ignored her and spoke to Sophie. "Was it you I saw out on the hills the other end of the village this morning?" Once again he was suspicious, and once again she had to remind herself that Toby Heron, his best friend, had told her to keep things to herself.

"Might have been," she said.

"With two boys?"

She shrugged, and his voice thickened. "I don't think that's a good idea."

Sophie saw colour rise in her mother's cheeks. "Why ever not?" Her voice was sharp. "They've always been together, all three."

"Oh, have they?" Distaste swam in his glamorous eyes. "Well, in my opinion I don't think they should."

"She's my daughter. I'm the one she'll talk to about her friends!"

Sophie's skin prickled to hear her mother fighting back at last, but she feared the effect it might have.

He sat where he was and stroked the table-cloth with both hands like a man who had to prevent himself sweeping all the dishes to the floor with his thick arm. But his expression was as placid as ever.

"They'll be no good," he said. "Those two boys aren't the least bit of use."

"Yes they are!" cried Sophie. "You don't know them!"

When he stood up the kitchen seemed to shrink. They were too close to him. "Keep her here," he said to Sophie's mother. "You never know what's out there on the hills."

"What do you mean?" The haunted look returned to Lucy Nelson's face. "Is it an animal?"

He remained silent for a long moment, and then he said, "She knows what I mean. She knows very well, and those two boys know it. They know it as well as I do, and they aren't big enough to protect her." He moved to go out. "I've got things to do, and you ..." he turned slowly towards Sophie, "while you are a guest in my house you will stay indoors."

Sophie watched through the window until the pick-up had swung out of the gateway and headed towards the village. Reg Boston had a secret. She had known it ever since he had asked about the train. He had been far too interested, and she turned around to tell her mother about it despite her promise to Toby Heron, but Lucy Nelson spoke first.

"What did he mean, Sophie?" She was angry with Reg Boston, but she was also worried.

"He only wants to stop me going down to the village."

"But why?"

Now was her chance to speak about the train, but her mother's face was so anxious Sophie could not bring herself to trouble her with mysteries. She had to see the boys before anything else happened. Reg Boston suspected something and wanted to prevent them getting together.

"Mum," she said suddenly, "do you know what I think?" She was grinning, taunting her mother, anything to drive away the clouds that were gathering in Lucy Nelson's mind. "He wasn't talking about an animal out there – he was talking about something else, and you're scared of it as well."

"Scared of what?" There was almost a smile on her mother's face.

"You're scared of the Starveling Boy!"

And her mother laughed. "Oh, no I'm not!"

"Oh, yes you are. It's just before Christmas and that's the time the Starveling Boy knocks at people's windows."

Over a hundred years ago a ragged boy had walked into the village begging for food, but many houses had turned him away, and then there had been a robbery. He was blamed and he ran off into the snow. He could not have got far, but he was never seen again. He had crept into some hiding place in the hills and died. Now the Starveling Boy came back to haunt the village at Christmas.

"My mum's a coward!" cried Sophie. "She

daren't go anywhere when the Starveling Boy's around, not even down to the village with me."

"Oh, daren't I!"

"Scaredy-cat!" Sophie made as if she was about to be chased around the table.

"I'll show you who's a scaredy-cat!" A glint of mischief was in Lucy Nelson's face, and they raced each other to put on their boots and coats. It was like old times, and they linked arms as they followed the tracks of the pickup into the village.

It was getting dark, and as daylight slipped away the single street lamp of Lott's Bend seemed too small and fragile to battle with the coming night. But the sparkle of Christmas trees in windows turned rooms into warm caves in the snow, and some houses had lit candles on their doorsteps and the flames were as steady as frost in the still air.

They met Simon outside the store. "My father sent me down to fetch his mobile phone," he said. All the lines were down and it was the only usable telephone in the village. "Everyone wants it," said Simon, "and Mr Thomas in there has been using it to see if he can get supplies." Through the panes of the store window they could see the shopkeeper talking to customers but not doing much business.

"We'd better go and see if there's anything

left." Lucy Nelson went inside, but Sophie lingered.

She began to tell Simon about how Toby Heron had asked them to say nothing about the train, but Simon had already made up his mind that no one would hear about it from him.

"Don't worry," he said. "Toby Heron's another one like Jack – he'll believe anything. But didn't you tell him that the man's car had stuck in a snowdrift and he'd walked along the cutting?"

"I didn't have time."

She felt foolish, but Simon had shrugged it aside and was telling her about how his mother had bought the ten shilling note. "Here's your share," he said, and he also gave her the money for Jack. "Now I've got to get home to get this phone charged up again. My mother keeps trotting round to all the neighbours with it and I can't think what it's going to be like on Christmas Day with everyone wanting to ring up people all around the world." He held it up to his ear and squeaked, "Hello, Granny – happy Christmas!"

She found Jack in the garage handing new plugs to his father, who was working on a tractor that had broken down while helping to dig through the snowdrifts.

"They reckon they was well on the way to getting through, Jack boy," said Mr Smith, "but when they come to the Devil's Elbow along by Scalybank there was a bit of an avalanche and that put 'em right back to where they begun. They say they've never seen anything like it up there."

"What about tomorrow?" Jack asked.

"Depends what comes." His father laughed. "Reckon they ought to bring in that train you saw."

"Give over, Dad." Jack turned away, red-faced. "I was just having you on. We never really saw a train, did we, Sophie?"

"Didn't sound like that when you first told me." Mr Smith looked over his shoulder at Sophie. "What d'you say, gal?"

"It was just a game, Mr Smith."

He rested his oily hands on the tractor wheel and looked from one to the other, a sparkle in his eyes. "Well, I can tell you it got a bit of a laugh over at the Blacksmith's when I told them."

Now she knew what had made Jack change his mind about the train, but her face was so startled at the thought that the secret was out that Jack's father laughed again.

"You ain't got nothing to worry about, my beauty," he said kindly. "They all knew you was just having a good time. Even that sour old character you helped bring in had to smile." Sophie and Jack exchanged glances, but stayed quiet.

"And by the way, Sophie," said Mr Smith, "I had a word with that old chap and he was very apologetic about the ten bob note and he said he'd make it right with you, so you ain't got nothing to worry about."

"The money doesn't matter any more," she said and handed over Jack's share, much to Mr Smith's amusement. He turned back to his work, and Sophie stayed silent. She had to talk with the other two before she gave anything else away.

Jack's father, tightening a plug in its socket, said, "I don't know about you, Sophie, but I never found Reg Boston had much conversation in him."

"No, he hasn't, Mr Smith."

"Keeps hisself to hisself, pretty well – that's always been my view of him."

"Yes," she said, wanting to let him know what she really thought of Reg Boston but not knowing how to do it.

"Well, you two womenfolk must've had some effect since he took you in. He's over at the Blacksmith's right now and talking a right load of old drivel."

"Thank you, Mr Smith," she said primly, and he laughed.

"Jack ain't the only one to open his mouth and put his foot in it," he said.

"Learnt it from you," said Jack.

While they beamed at each other, two of a

kind, Sophie risked saying, "Reg Boston told my mum he doesn't want me out in the snow with Jack and Simon."

"Did he, now? Well, I don't know about that, but I do know that when that stranger reckoned he'd seen footprints in the snow on the platform of the old station he stirred something up."

"Fox," said Jack. "Must've been a fox."

"That's what I say, but Reg Boston mumbled something to hisself, like he often do, and when the stranger asked him what he'd said I reckon the drink must have gone to Reg's head because he reckoned the footprints might have been the Starveling Boy! And I'd always took him to be an intelligent man – and that's right, ain't it, Sophie? Reg Boston is no one's fool."

She nodded. It was true.

"Well, the stranger gave him a right old-fashioned look, I can tell you, but that set them off, and they got to talking like they'd known each other for years – and that ten bob came up again, so I kept my ears open. Seems he's a bit of a collector and likes to have money of all sorts, going way, way back in time 'just in case', I heard him say. Just in case of what I couldn't make out." Mr Smith turned to look at them. "They was still going at it when I left to come home, which is a mighty strange way for Reg Boston to carry on … thick as thieves with someone he don't know."

NIGHT WALK

Deep in the night Sophie opened her eyes. Something had awakened her, some soft sound like the secret rustle of wrapping paper on Christmas Eve, but now that she was awake it had stopped. She listened. The house was asleep, but she was certain something had moved.

She slid from the warmth of her bed and went to the window. She could tell by the flakes that came ghosting close to the glass that the snow had come again, but further away among the trees the falling snow was invisible and nothing stirred in the white parkland of Heron Hall.

Then, from outside, the sharp crack as a frozen door opened made her jump. It came from the porch below her but no light sprang out, and when the door was nudged shut she held her breath as a dark figure moved out from the shadow of the porch roof.

Reg Boston was moving cautiously, pushing his feet through the snow, not lifting them clear, making certain that his footfalls were muffled. He disappeared around the corner of the house and she waited to hear the sound of his pick-up truck being started, but nothing happened. Her room was cold and she guessed it was long after midnight but she could not go back to bed. She had to see where he was going.

She dressed quickly. There was no sound from her mother's room, and she went down to fumble for her anorak and boots in the dark, and when she tried the outside door it opened noiselessly. She let the snowflakes settle on her face as she looked out. The house was ringed near and far by the upright black shadows of trees, but there was no sign of Reg Boston.

She stepped out and pulled the door closed. Now she was a night creature, a shadow herself, and she saw where he had gone. She trod in his tracks to the corner of the house.

The truck was where he always left it and there was no silhouette of a man inside the cab, and no figure moved in the driveway to the Hall. She stooped and saw that his trail led towards the gates and the road. He had left the house determined to make no noise and was heading for the village on foot.

The road had been kept open as far as the gates of the Hall but the track was narrow between the heaped hedges. Boston must have gone that way, and the distance had swallowed him. There would be no escape for her if he turned back, but once she had started she began to run, panting and stumbling.

After a while she stopped and listened. There was no sign of him, and she ran on until the church at the edge of the village came in sight. It stood alone on a patch of rising ground, and the churchyard wall curved around the last bend into the village street. She saw him as he came out of the shadow of the wall and began to walk into the village.

She reached the corner of the churchyard and watched. The housefronts were all in darkness and he kept close to one side of the street as he neared the single street lamp that was strung between the rooftops of the Blacksmith's Arms and the store. Snow had so caked its glass that it was no more than a handful of pale light and she was having difficulty keeping him in sight when, from above her, the church clock rang out the hour and startled her into looking up. Two strokes and then silence.

She turned once more towards the patch of light and saw him. But he was no longer alone. Someone had joined him and together they were already disappearing into the shadows of the houses ahead.

Sophie moved after them. The second figure was shorter, but the black hat and overcoat gave him away. The stranger had let himself out of the inn, and he and Reg Boston were heading out into the darkness.

She reached the patch of light and her footsteps became leaden. It was not tiredness. It was her courage that was beginning to fade. Once she had put the village behind her there was nothing ahead but the snowbound pass, and she could not follow two men out into the loneliness of the bleak hills.

Suddenly she drew the icy air into her lungs. They could not be going far. She knew exactly where they were heading, and she knew what she had to do.

Jack was close by. The blacksmith's house was joined to the old forge, and Jack's front door was in a narrow passageway at the side. But Sophie passed by the door and went through a little gate into the garden at the back. Jack's window was blank and the frozen garden was silent. She felt she was a ghost playing a ghostly game as she stooped to make a snowball and throw it at his window. She missed, but her second throw hit the pane and before it slid to the bottom so did her third. She had the fourth in her hand when the curtain drew to one side and the pale smudge of a face showed through the glass. There was a moment of panic. Perhaps it was not Jack. She was ready to run, but she waved and it could only have been Jack who waved back before he let the curtain fall.

He was quick. The door in the passageway opened softly and he put his boots outside and stepped into them before he spoke. "Where are we going?" He snuffled like a badger, still half asleep.

"The station," she said.

"Great." He didn't ask why, but she told him.

"And they can't be going anywhere else," she said.

He nodded and zipped up his windcheater. They both knew there was nowhere else to go. "I've still got my pyjamas on underneath," he said.

"So have I."

They looked at each other from under their hoods. In pyjamas. In the village street with the snow tickling their cheeks. They had slipped into some strange Christmas dream.

They had to be cautious. At the end of Station Lane they gazed into the long avenue of trees and could see no sign of the two figures. They stooped to examine the snow. There was not enough light to be certain of footprints, but the snow had definitely been scuffed.

"I wish Simon was here," said Jack. Simon would have had a torch.

The avenue had too many shadows for them to make out what lay ahead, and as they went forward they placed their feet carefully to prevent their boots creaking as their feet pressed the snow and they breathed gently in case the mist of their breath should give them away.

The station yard was empty, but their eyes had become skilful in the lack of light and they could make out that a double trail went straight across to the steps leading up to the entrance to the platform. They halted. They would show up too clearly if they attempted to cross the open space, but they had to find some way of following.

Sophie shivered. She had been walking through the night for a long time and her feet and fingers were numb. She hardly felt Jack's tug at her arm. He pointed.

Through the station entrance they could see a section of the snow-covered platform, and against the whiteness shadows were moving. "It's them," he whispered, and as they watched they saw that the two figures were walking to and fro along the platform, waiting for something, keeping themselves warm. When they vanished behind the ticket office Sophie nodded to Jack and they ran. She reached the steps first and crouched. She could hear the men's footsteps crackle in the frozen snow, but their words were muffled.

"Someone's got to get closer," she whispered,

and Jack began to move forward but she pulled him back. "No," she said, "it's got to be me." She was smaller and more nimble, and she eased herself up the steps and in two paces had placed herself with her back to the ticket office door.

"I don't see the need." It was Boston's voice.

Then words were lost in the shuffle of the footsteps before she heard the stranger "... if your timetable is anything like accurate, friend Reginald, then the night mail is due through here any minute now."

"And if it doesn't stop I'm off back to my bed. I've done my part already."

The stranger was laughing as they passed the opening and she missed what was said next, but Boston must have continued to complain because the stranger was encouraging him as they turned and walked back.

"... just as far as Scalybank Halt," he was saying. "It's less than a mile down the line and it could be useful to us. I'd like to see it tonight..." and then she heard no more, for the men fell suddenly silent and a flickering, weak light illuminated the platform. It was as though she was gazing at a stage in a theatre, and she pressed herself further into the shadow of the doorway as the scenery changed and the play began. A man walked along the platform, but he was not one of the two she had followed. He wore a peaked cap, and

50

carried an oil lamp.

He moved out of sight, and then there came a rumble and the clank and pant of machinery, a gush of steam and a train entered, juddered, slowed and stopped. Now all she saw was a row of carriage doors and faintly lit windows. There was a brief trundle of trolley wheels from somewhere out of sight along the platform, a carriage door slammed, the engine gave a full-throated cough of steam, the carriages slid by, and the darkness and silence fell into place once more.

When she and Jack crept forward the platform was bare. The man with the lamp was nowhere to be seen, and Boston and the stranger had vanished. The train had carried them away.

Sophie and Jack had nothing to say. The night was too huge and had too many mysteries. They would talk about it tomorrow ... if they still believed it. They would even tell someone; but now they had to get home.

Only an occasional moth of snow drifted around the light outside the Blacksmith's Arms, and Jack said he would walk with her beyond the curve of the churchyard wall and watch until she was within sight of the gatehouse. Then he found he could not turn his back on her as she dwindled into the white shadows and he ran after her.

"I'll go as far as the gate," he said, but still

they remained silent. It was as if the night had clamped their minds shut, and they were so tired they had to concentrate not to stumble in the ruts.

It was not until he had seen Sophie let herself into the gatehouse that he lifted his eyes to look at the sky. He was in a wilderness. Somewhere above the clouds there must have been a moon for he could see the fields blank and white and untouched. Nothing moved out there. He was alone, a tiny shape toiling in the trough of the lane when he should have been at home, in bed. Nothing else was wandering through the night.

In the cold air his eyelashes were stiffening with ice and he raised a hand to brush them. As he did so it seemed that beyond his fingers, out on the smooth surface of the field, there was a movement. He lowered his hand. It was nothing more than a few spindly branches at the top of a hedge. Nothing had stirred.

He ploughed on, concentrating on the track, refusing to turn his head, but he could not stop himself looking from the corner of his eye. Something seemed to be keeping pace with him.

He stopped and turned. By facing it he would kill the illusion stone dead.

But the figure kept moving. On thin legs it picked its way through the snow like a deer. But it was no deer. It was upright, human, and as if it was aware that it had been spotted, it changed direction and made towards him.

Jack ran. He stumbled often, his feet seemed clogged as if the track was closing on him like a vice, and all the time the figure came slanting across the field.

At the churchyard wall he fell. He rolled on his back, his mouth ready to yell, and he bent his legs ready to kick and fight.

And nothing happened. No sound. Not a whisper of wind. Nothing but the frozen night. Nothing … except that over the churchyard wall a thin grey face was looking down on him.

He scuffled sideways, got to his feet and ran into the village not caring what noise he made, but nowhere did any lights come on, and even when the door of his house clumped shut behind him no one awoke.

SECRETS AND LIES

Reg Boston's smile put attractive creases at the corners of his eyes. It was then that Sophie hated him most. "You two girls need a good breakfast on a morning like this," he said. He was busy at the stove with bacon and eggs.

Lucy Nelson was wary of him but the smile had done its work. "Smells delicious," she said and turned to Sophie. "What do you think, sleepyhead?"

"Oh, don't!" Sophie shut her eyes. "I'm not three years old."

Lucy glanced at Reg Boston. "I think she must have had a sleepless night."

"I did." Now was the time to say it ... while her mother was smiling at him. "I was wide awake," she said. "I couldn't sleep so I got out of bed." He was watching her, and in spite of herself she had the urge to yawn. She forced herself to speak. "I went to the window and looked out." She waited. He must have known what she meant. The eggs in the skillet sizzled and spat. "It was after midnight," she said.

"Then you must have seen me." He was calm and his expression was serious. He was about to tell them what had happened in the night. Her nerves tautened, and again she had to struggle not to yawn. "Did you see me?" he said.

"Yes."

"Then I'm sorry I woke you, Sophie. I tried not to."

"I know." And he had been quiet enough not to waken her when he returned.

Lucy Nelson glanced from one to the other. "I feel quite left out of it," she said. "Nothing woke me." But something troubled her. "I hope it's not because of us, Reg, disturbing all your routines."

"There was nothing routine about last night." He began to put food on their plates. "I hoped you would never find out." He put a plate in front of Sophie. "Something's going on."

Now it would all come out – the train, everything. Sophie stiffened. Her mother drew in her breath sharply. She was very pale.

"I went out last night ..." he spoke slowly, dragging out his words, "because there is something out there in the snow ... and I have to make sure it doesn't come anywhere near

55

the house." Sophie lifted her head and faced the full charm of his smile. "I have to look after my two young women."

"But, Reg," her mother was filled with anxiety, "what can it be? Is it an animal?"

He shrugged, and Sophie saw that he was satisfied. His lie was distracting her mother from thinking clearly. "Animal?" he said. "Maybe. Maybe not."

"You mean it may be human?" Lucy Nelson's eyes were wide.

He pretended to make light of it. "Well, you know the story that they tell at this time of the year," he was chuckling, "it could be that."

"The Starveling Boy?" Lucy Nelson suddenly lost patience. "Be serious, Reg, for goodness' sake and tell me what's out there!"

"Don't worry, Lucy. You are quite safe so long as neither of you goes out alone after dark."

So that was it. The lie was to keep them indoors and leave Reg Boston and the stranger to get on with whatever was happening in the night.

There was a crunch of footsteps outside and a rap on the door. Toby Heron was there, red-faced with the cold and grinning with excitement. Sophie saw that he was using it to disguise his suspicion of Reg Boston. "There's a helicopter coming!" he said. "It's going to get here between the snowstorms and we've got to clear a landing pad."

News had just reached him from Simon's father that the helicopter was to try to land in the grounds of Heron Hall. "It's on its way now," he said. "We need every shovel we've got!"

Boston threw some tools into the pick-up truck, but Toby hung back, and the excitement he had put on for Boston's benefit left his face. "There are many strange things happening, isn't that so, Sophie?" He kept his eyes on her until he was certain she understood there was still a secret between them.

She nodded and said quietly, "Lots of strange things." And much stranger than even Toby knew.

"It's almost better than Christmas!" It was the kind of thing Jack would have said, but Toby had taken a risk. Boston had seen the glance that passed between them and was curious. "What's this helicopter bringing?" he asked. "Food?"

"It's not bringing anything, Reg. It's for poor Mrs Morton. She's not too well and they've got to get her to hospital. We'd better hurry. How much space does a helicopter need?"

They piled into the pick-up and drove to the lawn in front of the Hall. They were still sweeping a wide circle clear when there was a clatter in the sky and the yellow machine came over the hilltops and dropped down towards them.

The rotors stirred up an instant blizzard through which the crewmen carried old Mrs Morton, bundled up in so many blankets she could hardly be seen, into their machine. They were returning for her husband, and all eyes were watching, when Sophie felt a tug at her sleeve and looked round to see Toby Heron stooping towards her. Through the swirl of snow and noise he mouthed the words: "Come up to the Hall to see me as soon as you can. Tell your mother anything you like – say I've got some apples for you. But come alone."

"What about the boys?"

"How much do they know?"

"Everything."

"Bring them!"

THE HIDDEN WORKSHOP

Toby Heron let them into the Hall just as Reg Boston went out at the back to his pick-up parked among the outbuildings. "He didn't see you as you came up the drive, did he?" Toby asked.

"I don't think so," said Sophie. They had been careful. "He knows too much already."

Toby was gazing out of a window alongside the front door. "Knows too much, does he?" he said to himself. "I wonder what makes young Sophie say that."

As he said "young Sophie" she raised her eyebrows and pulled a face at the boys.

"There he goes," said Toby, and they looked past him to see the truck going down the drive towards the gatehouse. "I have great respect for Reg," he said. "You have to admit he got that landing pad cleared for the chopper in double-quick time." He paused, keeping his eyes on the retreating truck. "Your mother's very fond of him, Sophie."

"She's frightened of him." The words came out so easily she realized she had been wanting to tell somebody about it for a long time. "So am I," she said.

"Frightened. Is that a fact?" He turned away from the window quite slowly, but as he did so he seemed to become more bulky and his face was no longer cheerful. The cheerful plumpness had darkened, and with a shock they saw that Toby Heron was not always as gentle as he seemed. "Has he harmed you?" His voice had a hard edge.

"No." She had to speak carefully. "But he wants to keep us in the house … if he can."

"If he can!" Toby Heron suddenly changed. He laughed. "I believe this girl can run rings round our friend Reg!"

Sophie blushed. "He knows about the train," she said, and was about to tell him more, but his manner had changed yet again and he was not listening.

His questions had ceased as abruptly as they had begun. He was still wearing his outdoor clothes and he took off his crumpled hat and rubbed the back of his head, thinking. He made up his mind, and suddenly turned back to the window, gazing down the drive where Reg Boston was no longer in view, and rapped out orders over his shoulder.

"Library!" he snapped. "You know where it is. Kick the snow off your boots."

They obeyed. Everyone in the village knew the ins and outs of Heron Hall, so they opened the tall double doors of the library and went through. The library windows overlooked the snow scene of the parkland, and Toby Heron glanced once more towards the gatehouse before he turned his attention to the three who stood in front of the big log fire.

"Coats off if you're too hot. Sit down." Once more they obeyed. "Now, Sophie ..." he threw his hat on the floor and sat facing them in a high-backed armchair "... tell me all you know about the train."

She glanced at the others to apologize. "I know we promised not to tell anyone, but it just slipped out when I was talking to Mr Heron yesterday."

"Toby," he said. "And don't worry about secrets between the four of us. I shall have a few secrets to tell you before you leave this house."

He looked at each of them in turn. They all had something to say, but when the story of the train had been told he sat brooding so deeply they fell silent. Then Toby Heron straightened. "I'm a man with a problem," he said. "And you three are it." He frowned as if he wished they would go away. "You know too much."

Jack said, "You can't blame us for that."

Toby stood up. "And you, Jack Smith, are in it deeper than anyone – little though you know it." He glared at Jack as though he was angry with him. "You and I go so far back in this dreadful business that I am going to have to tell you, all three of you, things I would rather keep to myself."

"So what have I done?" Jack was ready to argue.

"Not much. Not yet." Toby's gaze suddenly switched to Sophie and he snapped at her. "You don't like my best friend, do you?"

He seemed to be accusing her, and she did not answer.

"You know who I mean – Reg Boston! You think he's a cheat. You think he's a liar."

Her eyes were wide, not understanding, and he swung away.

"Well, that's what he is! A cheat and a liar. And you proved it." He began to pace to and fro, and she saw that his anger was not directed at her but at Reg Boston. "He steps in front of me at every turn! I would have rescued you and your mother from the snow, but he gets there first. You could be living here, and I would –" He broke off as if he feared saying too much. "What I mean to say, Sophie, is that it isn't the first time he has gone behind my back. He has stolen things from me that I would have gladly shared with him and now, because he knows that I suspect him, he has joined forces with an old enemy of mine to rob me."

He paused, and Simon dared to say what they all thought. "Well, why don't you throw him out?"

"There's too much at stake! Isn't that obvious!" Toby pulled up short, startled by his own anger. He waved a hand as if to wipe it out. "You are not to blame," he said. "I am frustrated because we are alone, cut off by the snow, and there's danger. The three of you have stumbled into something that should never have troubled you."

"Well, why don't you tell someone else?" said Simon and, after a moment, the ghost of a smile appeared on Toby's face.

"Other people aren't like you," he said. "They would take a lot of convincing. And once the secret was out, then Reg Boston and my enemy would destroy every scrap of evidence to keep themselves in the clear and everyone would think I was mad."

"The train would never come again and no one would ever believe you," said Sophie quietly. "Except us."

Toby smiled at her. "I've already said you know too much."

Simon remained aloof. He had not been with the other two in the middle of the night, and although Jack had told him everything on their way up from the village to see the helicopter he still felt left out of it when they spoke about the train gliding along the platform as though it had been on a stage.

"Sounds more and more like a pantomime to me," he said. "It's a trick." He turned to Toby. "It's not a real train, is it?"

Toby gazed into the fire for a moment before he answered. "I believe you are a scientist, Simon."

"I try to be." Simon did not get too many compliments, so spots of colour appeared in his cheeks. "Everything must be tested."

"So it should. There's nothing more exciting than a doubt."

"Good." Simon was satisfied. "So, as it obviously is not a genuine train it must be a trick. What's the explanation," he hesitated, "Toby?"

"I'm not clever enough to tell you how a trick like that could be done, Simon." Toby got to his feet. "But I can show you how a real train came into the station last night."

He went to the bookshelves alongside the fireplace and took down a volume. "My great-great-grandfather Silas was a very meticulous man," he said. "He liked to keep everything in order, and he wrote a very careful diary ... but I expect you know that."

They did. Silas Heron's diaries were often talked about by people in the village, especially the older ones, who read about their own ancestors in what the inhabitant of Heron Hall had written in his journals of a century and more ago.

"Well, old Silas had all his diaries bound in the same way." The volume Toby held was bound in leather with gold tooling, and on the spine was a single figure. "Volume Three, as you see. Which is strange, because if you were to look inside Volume Four you would see that the two books seem to be in the wrong order. The dates don't follow on properly. And it's the same with all the other volumes. It drives people mad."

"I know," said Simon. His mother had looked through them.

"Twenty-five volumes," said Toby, "and all numbered neatly and all placed in the correct order on the shelf just as he left them. But they don't run in the order he wrote them. Volume Three near the beginning should be right at the end of the row because it was written in the year 1901, which was nearly at the end of his life."

They could see that the numbering ran correctly from 1 to 25.

"All wrong," said Toby. "The years are jumbled up, no rhyme or reason at all. Yet he was a very tidy man – as Jack may very well know."

Once more Jack was mystified.

"Your father will know," said Toby Heron, but he had not yet finished with the diaries. "Quite a long time ago I got to thinking about these strange volumes and one day it occurred to me to –"

"– put them in order," Simon interrupted. "Put them in date order and see if he meant anything by it."

Toby nodded. "A scientific experiment," he said, and he began taking down volumes and putting them in different places. "It took me a little time, but I have memorized the correct order according to the dates, and there it is." He stood back.

"So?" Simon was dissatisfied.

"So watch this." Toby Heron put out a hand towards the books, but instead of grasping one of them he gripped the shelf itself and gave it a tug. A whole section of the bookcase swung towards him. "Old Grandfather Silas was well aware that lots of libraries had doors disguised with books," he said, "but he wanted his door to be really secret, so he gave it a special sort of lock."

"Those books are all different thicknesses." Simon was working it out. "So they must fit into special places at the back of the shelves. They are just a key, a big key, and when they're in the proper order they open the lock! Simple."

"Glad you think so," said Toby, and saw

the other two grin. "Maybe you'll be able to help me out when we come to the really hard part."

"I'll do my best," said Simon.

The space behind the shelves was in darkness until Toby picked up a table lamp and went through trailing a long lead. "My great-great-grandfather used oil lamps," he said, "and I've left it just as I found it."

They were in a small, windowless chamber that, like the library, was lined with bookshelves. But there was a difference: the books were few, and the shelves carried many small mechanisms, many of which were obviously clocks, but others with unusual arrangements of delicate cogs and brass rods, thin spirals, dials and pendulums. And several that seemed incomplete stood on a bench amid a scatter of tools.

"Grandfather Silas's workshop," said Toby. "It was never a complete secret, but it was certainly private and it had been forgotten until I went looking for it."

"It looks secret enough to me," said Jack and was surprised that this made Toby chuckle.

"Well, he couldn't have made this room by himself, Jack. Who do you think was the most likely person to have helped him?"

Jack shrugged, but Sophie had the answer. "The blacksmith," she murmured.

Jack knew she was right, but there was something else. "Clocks," he said, and Toby Heron nodded.

"Your great-great-grandfather and mine," said Toby. "They worked together. Old Jack Smith had all the skill with his hands that old Silas Heron lacked. They worked together on all of these things. So now you know how Jack Smith, then and now, comes to be involved." He picked up a sheaf of dog-eared papers. "It's all here. He called this his Workbook, and it never left this room."

Jack's father was still pretty good with clocks and Jack said so, but Toby had more to tell them.

"Listen to me." He was no longer smiling. "Grandfather Silas was mad about time. Some people thought he was just plain, simple, ordinary mad in his head, which was why he eventually hid all his work away in this place so that people wouldn't be able to talk about it. But there came a day when he thought they were right and he really had gone completely mad." He leafed through the papers. "He invented a timepiece that was so accurate it always told the wrong time."

"What?" Simon was frowning, but Toby held up a hand to prevent him interrupting.

"This timepiece was certainly very accurate, the most accurate he had ever made, but very often it instantly went wrong as soon as he had taken the very greatest pains to get it exactly right. And it wasn't wrong by a second or two … or a minute … it was often wrong by hours."

He glanced down at the papers. "One day he was in the library and his manservant brought in a tray with something for him to eat. When the man left, Grandfather Silas wound up his timepiece, which was quite large, set it right by the clock on the mantel over the fire and then went to the tray to pour himself some tea. But the teapot was empty and cold, there were dregs in the teacup, and the crumbs on the plate showed that his beef and bread had been eaten. Of course, he called his man back and told him he had brought an empty tray from the servants' hall, but the man was very indignant and called the cook to prove that he had brought in a full tray an hour ago."

"He must have fallen asleep," said Simon.

"That's what everyone believed – including Grandfather Silas himself. He checked his timepiece by the clock on the mantel and they agreed, so he must have gone to sleep after he had eaten his meal. He had made such a fuss that he felt guilty and went along to the kitchen to apologize … but then he discovered something very odd."

Toby looked again at the papers. "It was so odd he wrote it all down in detail. He discovered that his very accurate timepiece was an hour ahead of the kitchen clock, and an hour ahead of every other clock in the house ... *except* for the mantel clock in the library."

"So he had made a mistake." Simon was becoming impatient. "He had set the library clock an hour fast, and then he'd set his time-piece by it."

"Not quite," said Toby. "He had made a mistake when he was setting his new time-piece, and somehow it had made the mantel clock agree with it. They were both an hour wrong, and that was the hour that the servant insisted he had spent eating his beef and falling asleep. Yet he was certain he had done none of those things. It was just as if he had skipped an hour. He seemed to have stepped from one time to another. It set him thinking."

"I should think it did." Simon was sarcastic.

"It was very hard to believe," Toby agreed, "even for Grandfather Silas – but he did exper-iments and wrote them all up in these papers."

There was a silence and Sophie glanced at Jack. Ever since the secret door had opened she had seen that he had stepped into a different world. It showed in his face; he could believe in anything. But she herself would far rather have never seen the hidden room; Reg Boston was somehow connected to it. And when the silence was broken by Simon he brought an extra chill to the shadows of the little room.

"I've heard of this before," he said.

"How?" Toby was startled. "The Workbook has never left this room."

"I didn't even know it existed." Simon was certain of himself. "But I do know that things like that can happen. It is scientifically possible."

No one contradicted him, and he lifted his chin.

"My father and I talk about it. Strange things happen in physics when you try to look at very tiny particles, and time is never what you think it is. Some people think there can be parallel worlds running along side by side, so maybe it's possible to switch from one to the other. My father will be very interested when I tell him."

"No!" Toby Heron suddenly towered over him. "That you will never do!"

For a moment Simon quailed, but then he recovered and seemed about to argue. Toby stood back and his voice became softer.

"I am asking you to wait," he said. "If you speak out now we shall never learn the truth. Some things will be hidden for ever."

Simon sniffed, and then decided to back down. At least he had made his point. "If it's got anything to do with that train we thought we saw, I won't say a word to anyone. I wouldn't be so stupid."

Toby lowered his head and grunted. "That

train," he said, "is part of it. My great-great-grandfather travelled on it."

"How?" Sophie asked before Simon could butt in. It was impossible.

"He found that his new timepiece, once he had set it by some other clock, could make jumps in time, always backwards to something that had already happened, never forwards. But after a while he got tired of playing tricks in Heron Hall and decided on bigger things."

"The railway station!" Jack broke in. "The clock in the ticket office."

"That's the one." Toby chuckled. "He could go to the station with his timepiece, set it right by the station clock and quite suddenly wind his timepiece backwards to the time of yesterday's trains, or even much further back than that. And it would work all the way along the little branch line that runs through Lott's Bend…"

"The line that doesn't exist any longer," said Simon.

"Only three stations on it," said Toby, "and all of them now deserted, like Lott's Bend."

"So if you choose your time when there aren't many people around – like now, with all this snow – you can run a train that perhaps no one will see."

"And I know the place where he must have got on." Jack's mind was racing. "It's just the other side of the hills, so I don't suppose it's snowed in."

Questions began to pour out, but Sophie knew more than the other two. She remembered the surprise on Toby Heron's face when she had first told him they had seen the train. "So it still works along the branch line," she said, and waited until he nodded before she added, "but you haven't got the timepiece, have you?"

He shook his head. "It vanished."

"That means someone else has it – and it still works."

"It still works," he repeated, "but not for much longer. Its power is limited. And that's why things are becoming urgent."

"So how did it go missing?"

"Old Silas only had himself to blame," said Toby. "He called it his Railway Timepiece, and although everyone knew he was very attached to it nobody had any idea what it could do. Nevertheless someone took it, and although his family thought they knew who it was there was never any proof."

"Who did they think stole it?" she asked.

"Well, it's vague, but there was a big wedding at Heron Hall and members of the family came from far afield – including some distant cousins, and it was one of them who was suspected. Grandfather Silas's wife, my great-great-grandmother, found this cousin in the library reading his diary when he had no right to be there, and there was a scene. She ordered this cousin out of the house, and the Railway Timepiece must have gone with him because it was never seen again. All I have is Grandfather Silas's railway timetable for 1899."

He led them out of the workroom to an elegant little writing desk in the library. "This belonged to my great-great-grandmother," he said. "She kept the timetable in here. When I was younger I used to look at it and wonder." He opened the drawer, but it was empty. He was pulling open the other drawers, thinking he had made a mistake, when footsteps sounded in the corridor.

"Quick!" He hurried them back to the workroom, thrust them inside, flung their coats in, and shut the shelves on them.

They heard the library door open and Toby Heron say, "Oh, there you are, Reg. I expect you want me to do some more snow-shifting."

"Hardly that, Toby. I have something rather more important on my mind."

BEHIND THE BOOKS

Behind the shelves it was Sophie who realized the danger. Toby Heron was rearranging the diaries in the library as he talked to Reg Boston. "I've got to get these old books in the right order," he said, and they heard the hidden lock slip into place as Toby pushed the last volume into its position on the shelf. "I can't think how they came to be in such a muddle."

They had discovered narrow slots in the back of the shelves which gave them a view of the library, and they could see by Toby's face that he was deliberately wasting time. He was mouthing something at them as he kept his back to Reg Boston.

"Put the light on, would you, Reg?" he said loudly, but he shook his head and mouthed something they could not properly make out before he spoke very slowly and clearly, "It's too dark in this corner. Too dark."

And Sophie understood. He meant the lamp on its long trailing flex that lit the workroom. It was shining out through the slots. She moved quickly to switch it off, and Toby dropped a book with a clatter to disguise the sound. "I need a librarian in this place," he said.

"Never mind about that now." Boston was looking around the library. "Those three kids are hanging around somewhere. I saw them as I was coming up the drive."

Toby hardly hesitated. "I've sent them off to get some apples."

"Apples? What apples?"

"We have plenty in store, haven't we, Reg?" Toby was pleased with his quick thinking. "And people in the village need anything they can get this Christmas."

"That's their look-out." Boston had other things on his mind. "I've brought someone to see you, Toby."

A shadow that had been hovering at his back came into the open. Without his hat they did not at first recognize the stranger. His wiry grey hair was cropped close to his skull, and the harsh lines of his face were screwed into a smile that showed too many teeth.

"Apples!" he exclaimed. "What a kindly thought!" He held out his hand. "What a pleasure to meet you again after all these years!"

His small eyes, sitting on a staircase of wrinkles, shifted uncomfortably when he saw that Toby Heron did not recognize him, but he quickly recovered. "Toby!" he cried. "I'm your long lost kinsman ... your Cousin Will! May I offer you the hand of friendship?"

Reluctantly, Toby took his hand and said, "I'm very surprised to see you."

"And I would be surprised if you were not surprised." Cousin Will's confidence had returned. "There has been so much needless trouble between our two branches of the family." He drew in his breath and surveyed the room. "And this is where it all began so long ago. It is an appropriate place to put that unhappy affair behind us once and for all."

He began to stroll around the room examining the furniture, taking an interest in the books. "And it is pleasant to think that precious little has been altered over the years ... almost everything is as it was in the old gentleman's day." He almost tripped over a hole in the carpet and was very amused at that. "Even the original floor covering, Toby?"

"We haven't exactly prospered here in Lott's Bend," said Toby. "Others have done much better."

The little eyes looked sidelong at him, sharp and victorious. "It's the way of the world, Toby – some prosper while others decline."

"And misfortune strikes some but not others."

"Ah, yes." Cousin Will became solemn. "I had forgotten the little setback your branch of the family suffered in your great-great-grandfather's time."

"It was hardly a little setback, Cousin. Grandfather Silas lost all his money."

"Lost it? That sounds rather careless. Hadn't he heard of banks?"

"He had no use for banks. He did all his business in cash, and he kept all his fortune in gold sovereigns in his desk."

"He was very eccentric," said Cousin Will.

"He trusted people."

Cousin Will shook his head. "That was more than careless."

Toby looked as if he was about to disagree, but had to say, "Someone robbed him."

"A beggar lad, I believe."

"The Starveling Boy." Toby paused, mulling something in his mind, before he added, "It wasn't the only misfortune in the old man's life, Cousin Will."

The two men regarded each other steadily, and then the smile rearranged itself on Cousin Will's face and a chuckle bubbled thickly in his throat. "We are referring, are we not, to the unhappy affair of … the Railway Timepiece?"

"It went missing," said Toby. "It well-nigh broke the old man's heart."

"Time heals all things." Cousin Will dismissed it. "Old grievances should be put behind us: Whoever holds the Timepiece no doubt treasures it."

Toby grunted, looking at his feet. Then he raised his head. "You must have been in the village for some time, Cousin," he said. "I hope you had a good journey before the weather cut us off – the snow is very deep."

"Deep and crisp and even." Cousin Will spaced his words, still smiling. "A cold coming I had of it, but the journey itself was almost, shall I say … miraculous?"

Cousin Will was making no secret of who held the Railway Timepiece. They saw Toby's back stiffen and he turned away to say, "And what part did you play in all this, Reg?"

"You could say I began it all, Toby, but you've only yourself to blame." He glanced around the library shelves. "It's all here, under your own nose, but you neglected it. I was the one who did the research."

"When I wasn't watching."

Boston shrugged. "It all came down to the clock in the ticket office – that was the big breakthrough. I discovered that the clock and the Railway Timepiece worked together, so I wound up the old station clock, got it going and had a word with your cousin. Simple as that, Toby; you should have thought of it yourself."

"Without a word to me," said Toby.

"If I had mentioned it you would have done

nothing, Toby old friend." Boston was sneering. "You could never bring yourself to insult your cousin by asking if he had got his hands on something that went missing years ago. I did. You haven't the nerve."

Toby glanced at Cousin Will before his eyes again rested on Boston. "And I see you found someone who shares your way of looking at things."

"All's fair in love and war, Toby. If there's anything to be made out of all this we don't intend to cut it three ways after we have done all the work. If someone loses, someone gains." Boston raised his eyebrows. "I like it to be me, that's all."

"The act of a true friend," said Toby. He stared, wooden-faced, at Reg Boston, and neither of them moved.

Cousin Will had been watching them, and now he interrupted. "My dear Toby," he said, "I have come to Lott's Bend at Christmas to heal the rift between us by making a confession. I imagine you know what I have in mind." He had been shielding a small wooden case. Now he produced it. "I possess Grandfather Silas's Railway Timepiece – and here it is!"

Boston had moved a step forward in case Toby attempted to snatch it, but Toby remained motionless and allowed Cousin Will to place the case on the library table and unfasten its catches. The polished sides folded down and there stood the Timepiece. It was larger than a carriage clock, and nothing like so pretty. If there was a dial it was hidden away somewhere in an untidy web of brass struts and wheels, and few people would have guessed its purpose as a timekeeper.

From behind the shelves they could not see the expression on Toby's face, but Reg Boston gave him a pitying, superior smile and said, "It's all there, Toby. All you have to know is when a train is due, and you can take a trip back in time and catch it."

Suddenly Toby was laughing. "And you are expecting me to believe you can catch a train that ran a hundred years ago?" He held out a hand. "At least I know what became of the timetable in the desk. You'd better let me have it back, Reg, if it can help to work magic." He was still chuckling when Boston refused. "What I don't understand is why you are telling me all this. Why don't you just make a fortune with it?"

He was turning away when Cousin Will came forward. "The Railway Timepiece is yours." He paused and placed his hand on it. "On one condition."

It was as if he had not uttered a word. "If you will excuse me," said Toby, "I shall go to see how they are getting on with the apples." He opened the library door and stood aside for them to leave.

"What a great shame." Cousin Will shook his grey head. "I was afraid it would come to this. My kinsman is offended." He looked at Boston. "Has the moment arrived to tell him of your other discovery?"

"It seems we have no choice." Boston reached across Toby and closed the door. "Sit down, old friend." Toby remained where he was. "As you wish, but you've really brought it all on your own head." He stood back, amusement glinting in his eyes. "We know all about the other one!"

It did not have the effect he expected. "Other one?" Toby was mystified.

"The other timepiece. The one he was working on when he died. The timepiece that was ten times as powerful!"

And Toby Heron burst into laughter that this time was genuine. "So that's what's on your mind – the Midwinter Watch!"

They stayed silent until his laughter subsided, and then Boston drawled, "You are very careless, Toby. You should never have left the old man's notes lying around. I haven't had time to figure out where you have them hidden, but I caught a glimpse of them once and I read all about how he had to improve on that clumsy timepiece which could only operate on the railway. He was working on another one, much more powerful." He watched Toby's smile fade. "We want it."

"Who wouldn't?" said Toby. "But as it doesn't exist, you are wasting your time."

Cousin Will's voice had become silky. "Those papers would help us make up our minds."

"I'm sure they would." Toby was scornful. "And if you did lay your hands on the Midwinter Watch – I take it you have a particular use for it?"

Cousin Will's eyes held Toby's. "As to its particular use, I rather think you and I would have the same thing in mind." He paused. "Suppose … just suppose … we could use the Midwinter Watch to go back to the moment, the precise moment, when the beggar boy stole your Grandfather Silas's fortune." He raised his eyebrows. "That would be of interest, surely?"

"So you could see what happened to the loot? I follow your reasoning, Cousin. The thought had also occurred to me, but as the Midwinter Watch does not exist…" He let his voice trail away.

Cousin Will was not to be put off. "The money was never found," he said. "Grandfather Silas was never able to use the Watch to find out for himself."

"The shock of the robbery killed him."

"Quite. So perhaps now is the time to solve the mystery. It would be very satisfying."

"And profitable, of course, if the money turned up."

Cousin Will ignored Toby's sarcasm. "I think we shall have earned our reward."

"So the money would be stolen again," said Toby. "From me."

Cousin Will shrugged.

"The only trouble is," Toby continued calmly, "you have left it a bit late." He had their attention. "I have read the notes, too, and Grandfather Silas had something in mind when he gave the Watch its name. In spite of all his efforts the Midwinter Watch has one failing which it shares with that timepiece on the table, as you must know – after a certain date it surrenders all its power. And that date is almost upon us. There was nothing old Silas could do about it – both timepieces give up their power in the middle of winter ... at Christmas this year." He laughed. "So, after Christmas, that wonderful Midwinter Watch will become nothing in particular, just another old watch – if you ever find it. And you haven't much time."

"Nor have you!" Boston lurched forward. "I expected a little trouble from you, Toby, so I've made sure you will cooperate."

"Nothing will do that, Reg, my former friend. You've been wasting your time."

Boston hardly seemed to have been listening. "I wonder if you happened to notice that someone was missing when the helicopter landed?" he asked.

"You yourself weren't around all the time, I did notice that."

"And someone else should have been there, but wasn't. Whatever happened to Lucy Nelson? Why wasn't she with the rest of you? Didn't you notice she was missing – and she such a pretty woman? Shame on you, Toby Heron! Unfortunately for you, I have a way with the ladies, and she was happy to take a little trip with me. On a train."

"A train! What have you done!" Toby lunged at him and Boston backed away, fending him off. "Where is she!"

"I managed to make her take a trip down the line to Scalybank Halt. I left her there. It's a disagreeable little place in winter, but she's quite safe ... for the moment, at least."

Toby was about to lunge again, but saw it would be useless. In spite of himself, he glanced towards the shelves. Behind the books, Sophie pressed her knuckles to her mouth to prevent herself crying out.

Toby took a deep breath. "The Midwinter Watch does not exist," he said. "You are wasting your time." He turned his back on Boston and spoke directly towards the shelves. "I have searched for it over and over again but it is not to be found."

The message was for them as much as for

the two men, and Toby Heron meant it. There was no Midwinter Watch. But Reg Boston had not given up. He waited until Toby faced him. "I read about the Midwinter Watch in those papers. Get them!"

Toby began to move as if he was going to obey, and behind the shelves they held themselves rigid; the papers were beside them on the bench. But quite suddenly he stood rock solid and confronted his cousin. "You see nothing until I have proof that Lucy Nelson is safe!"

Boston stepped forward, but Cousin Will put out a hand. "Contain yourself, Reg. Let us hear him out."

"Take me to her." Toby kept his voice low. "And then you can have what you like."

"No go, Toby." Boston shook his head. "We haven't time for that."

And Toby suddenly put his hands behind his back and began pacing the room like a ship's captain on the bridge. He stopped near the shelves. "I'll make a bargain with you," he said. "I want proof that you can do what you say you can. You have got to show me you can reach Lucy Nelson out there in the snow." He spun around. "Or I will do nothing to help you, and you will never see those papers."

Cousin Will again had to silence Boston. "And how do you propose we prove it?"

"Take me to the station and show me that

86

that contraption," he nodded towards the Railway Timepiece, "can do what you say it does. You must show me a train." It was his last word. He turned his back on them and faced the shelves. The two men were still muttering together when he spoke again, directly to the three behind the books. "Do nothing," he mumbled, and immediately cleared his throat as if he had made a false start and began again as he turned to face the men. "I am ready to go with you," he said loudly. "Lead the way."

Boston's face clouded with anger at having to agree but he beckoned to Toby, and the three men left the library together.

THE PENDULUM

It was Simon who fumbled for the lamp switch and unlatched the bookshelf door. Sophie stepped into the library. It was no longer a place of books where an old man had studied clocks and watches; it was a hollow space where two smiling men had gloated over stealing her mother away.

Jack looked at her pale face and was surprised that she was not crying. "She's safe," he said. "Toby Heron will bring her back." He knew there was no certainty in it.

The tip of Sophie's tongue touched her dry lips but her voice was hoarse. "We've got to do something," she said. It was the one thing Toby had forbidden. "Why did he say do nothing!"

"He meant don't raise the alarm." Jack hated himself for saying it. "It might make things worse."

"How!" she cried, and her voice echoed uselessly in the long room.

There was silence until Simon said, "We could always try to find the Midwinter Watch before they get to it."

Sophie turned on him. "How would that help? It doesn't exist!"

Simon could think only of the untidy look of the Railway Timepiece. Any scientist would have to work to improve it. There had to be something. "If we had it we could bargain with them." He sounded doubtful.

"He's right." Jack, with his eyes on Sophie, nodded as if he meant it. It was a feeble hope but they had to try. "We'll search the workroom."

Simon led the way back through the bookcase. He was in his element. "First of all," he said, and went to the bench and picked up Grandfather Silas's secret papers, "we've got to study this."

The old man's pen had occasionally sputtered on the thick paper but his handwriting was clear enough and so were the many diagrams of clocks and parts of clocks. "It's all here," said Simon, "everything he ever made. Look at this." He bent over a drawing in brown ink that showed an elaborate cogwheel attached to some form of rocker. "What is it?"

"It's an escapement," said Jack. "It's the part of the clock that makes the tick."

Simon raised his eyebrows, surprised that Jack should know so much. Jack shrugged. He was the son of a mechanic. But Sophie was on edge.

"What's that got to do with anything?" She had lost patience with them. "It doesn't tell us where to find it!"

Still Simon lingered. There were words among the drawings, but they were so brief they were difficult to understand. One word, however, was often repeated and Simon murmured it. "Synchronicity," he pointed at the page, "there it is again. It means things happening at the same time."

But Jack was ahead of him "... like when people say synchronize your watches," and was glad to see Simon close his eyes as if he didn't need Jack to explain anything for his benefit.

"And look at this." Simon stabbed at the page where two words were written in a large, excited scrawl: "Synchronicity achieved!"

And beneath it, written in a more sober hand, Grandfather Silas had noted: "The new Watch is completed, and this day in my library I set it in motion in harmony with the Great Cycle which I have observed in the Stars. If my calculations are correct, the events of this Time in this House are absorbed by my Watch and can be recalled at each turn of the Great Cycle which takes 300 days to run each course. I calculate it will run in harmony with the Great Cycle until Christmas Day one hundred years from now when the Stars assume a different aspect and harmony will be lost. I write this in midwinter, so I propose that my Watch will be known as the Midwinter Watch, though none yet know the extent of its reach. My task is to keep my Watch running from midwinter to midwinter without a pause until proof of my theories is clear. Until then the Midwinter Watch can be mistaken for any other timepiece. When the case of my Watch next opens in this house we shall see what we shall see. Its secret rests in the lap of Time." And the notes broke off except for a scrawl across the bottom of the page "– and now to my much-neglected accounts!"

Jack glanced at Sophie. There was not much hope in finding a watch that could easily have been lost over the years. Toby Heron was right; the Midwinter Watch did not exist. But Sophie's head was bent over the papers, seeking feverishly for any sign of hope. There was nothing more in the notes except sketches for the outer appearance of watches and clocks of different shapes and sizes.

"Well, at least we know," said Simon, "that the Midwinter Watch works with the big timetable in the stars, and Heron Hall is the place where things happen."

And Jack had noticed one more thing.

"Wasn't he doing his accounts when he was robbed?" It all seemed to hang together, and they were not the only people to know it. Others had seen these papers. But Sophie had lost patience. She snatched up the table lamp and was peering into the dark corners of the workroom.

"It can't be anywhere else," she said. "It's got to be here!"

But Toby Heron had long ago searched the workshop and there was no completed clock or watch anywhere to be seen. To make matters worse Simon stood alongside her and said bleakly, "And if it was going to work, the Midwinter Watch had to be kept wound up for more than a century. I can't hear anything ticking."

The silence was intense, and when she saw Jack still studying the notes she was suddenly angry with him. "Put that down," she ordered. "You're wasting time." And when he seemed reluctant she reached to take the sheaf of papers from him. "They've got my mother!" she cried. "We've got to do something!"

Still he clung to the notes, infuriating her more than ever by gazing at designs for nothing more important than the decoration of clock faces and pendulums.

"Jack," she pleaded, "that's not going to help," but he pointed to the bottom of the page and said, "There's something odd about this."

She looked. It was no more than a scribbled doodle. "What about it?" she asked. "It's only a pendulum."

"Not exactly. Look." He put his finger on the top of the long pendulum rod and brought it down to the circular bob at the bottom. Then he drew his finger part of the way around the rim of the bob as if drawing a hook at the end of the rod. "The circle doesn't finish," he said. "The whole pendulum is more like a long capital J."

"I don't care." She dismissed it.

"But I've seen it somewhere before." He pointed again. "And look at that." His fingertip was on the pen marks inside the pendulum bob.

"It's a scribble."

"It's an S."

She looked again. "So it's an S."

"J and S," he said. "J.S."

"Your initials."

"And my great-great-grandfather's. He was Jack Smith as well. I've seen that drawing somewhere."

Simon had listened. "They also stand for Jack and Sophie," he said. "It doesn't amount to much. We'd better get out of here before they come back."

The snow had come again so thickly that the hills were blurred, and they had to bow their heads against it as they ran to the gatehouse.

The most recent footprints on the doorstep had already been covered, and inside there was no sign of her mother except for a note on the kitchen table. It said: "Gone down to the village with Reg. Back soon."

Sophie's eyes when she turned them on Jack were larger than he had ever seen them. "What about the police?" she said desperately. "Simon's father has a phone that works."

But they all knew that the snow had shut them in more surely than ever ... and Toby Heron had clearly asked them to do nothing.

"It's nearly dinner-time," said Jack. "I mean lunch." It was what Sophie would have called it and he was already feeling awkward at what he was about to say. "You can't stay here, Sophie. You'd better come home with me and have something to eat."

As he spoke he realized he would have to make up a story that his mother and father would believe, and in his thoughts he was taking her through the garage into the house when something leapt into his mind that made him snatch at her hand and give her no chance to refuse.

SWINGING
TOGETHER

Snowflakes fell on Sophie's eyelashes and Jack enjoyed watching her blink them away. She walked between the two boys as they made their way to the village through snow that fell so thickly they were in a white twilight at midday and were quickly becoming part of the whiteness themselves. If it had really felt like Christmas she would have enjoyed clinging to the boys' arms and allowing them to shelter her, but she thought of her mother and the snow became an enemy.

And smaller things also troubled her. She wondered how Jack could invite her to lunch without his mother asking questions she could not answer, but all he would say was, "Don't worry about it ... it's Christmas, and she'll be quite happy." But Sophie could tell by the way he was making them hurry that there was something else on his mind. He would not say what it was.

In the cold cave of his father's garage they gathered around the pot-bellied stove and let the melting snow make puddles under their boots.

Jack tackled what was worrying her. He looked to where his father was half inside a car and said bluntly, "Do you reckon Sophie can stay for dinner, Dad? It's a long walk back and she's very cold."

"Of course she can."

Jack looked smugly at Sophie. "Told you," he said.

"But you'd better see your mother first," said Mr Smith, and Simon laughed.

Jack remained where he was. "Dad," he said, "can we have a look at the toolbox?"

"What toolbox is that, Jack?"

"You know the one. Great-great-grandad's – his clock things."

"What on earth for?" When Jack merely shrugged he added, "All right, then … but be careful with that stuff."

Jack went to a bench in the corner and got Simon to help him lift a black-painted metal box from beneath it. It was padlocked but Jack knew where the key was kept and he opened it.

Simon stooped over it and blocked Sophie's view. "Treasure," he said. "This has got to be worth a bit."

Sophie managed a glimpse. The box was filled with trays of tools. The best you could say about them was that they were clean and glittered.

"Clockmaker's tools." Jack, like Simon, admired them. "Old Jack Smith did all the work for Mr Heron. He knew a lot."

"Is there a clock in there?" Sophie asked.

"No. Only tools." But Jack's attention was no longer on them. Instead he pointed to the inside of the lid. The black paint was scratched from much use, but among the random marks there were some that were not accidental. Towards one corner someone had scratched a little drawing.

Jack watched them examine it before he said, "Do you see what it is?"

"It's obvious," said Simon. "A grandfather clock. Just a sketch."

"Yes." Jack was excited. "But look closer."

"It's a bit like one of those drawings in the workshop papers, I suppose."

It was Sophie who spotted what Jack meant. "It's got the JS pendulum," she said. She could see the capital J with the long shaft and the curled snake of the S in the hook of the J. She squinted and bent closer. "And there's some writing."

"Read it," said Jack.

"It's a bit of a scrawl … but I think it says: JS Keep Time Turning."

"*Jack Smith keep time turning?* – his grammar could've been better," Simon couldn't help pointing out.

"Who cares?" said Sophie. "We all get things wrong."

"But it's not wrong!" Jack was grinning. "And it's much more than it seems. I can show you."

They had not seen Jack's father come closer. His voice made them jump. "Jack's right," he said. "He can show you." He stood there, wiping black grease from his hands and grinning at having startled them. "We've got that very clock in this house."

Jack nodded. He seemed disappointed at having been interrupted, but his father had taken over.

"That old clock stands on the landing upstairs where it has been ever since it was put there by my great-grandfather just after he made it. It's never been shifted by as much as an inch in all that time ..." he laughed "... even though the wife just longs to get her brush to all them cobwebs behind it. But old Jack Smith knew better than to let that happen, and he laid it down that it was never to be shifted or else it would go wrong and all his work would be wasted."

"Big clocks like that do get out of balance if they're moved," said Simon.

Jack's father nodded. "And I'll tell you

98

another thing. That clock have been so carefully set up it vary no more than a minute or so in a week, and all I have to do is adjust the pendulum by a fraction."

"Never the clockwork?" asked Simon.

Mr Smith laughed again. "I ain't ever seen the clockwork. That's all sealed up to keep out the dust, and I ain't ever had cause to disturb it."

"So you don't know exactly what's inside," said Simon. Something about the Midwinter Watch being hidden behind the dial was on his mind and he looked at Jack, but Jack shook his head. Simon was on the wrong trail.

"All I know about the inside of this old clock," said Mr Smith, "is that its tick is as strong as it ever was, and all I ever do is what my father and his father done before me – we wind it up once a week, set the hands right if they're a wee bit out, which they hardly ever are, and leave well alone." He winked at his son. "It'll be your job one day, Jack. It's a tradition."

Jack did not want to think about that. "Can we go and look at it?" he asked.

"What, with them wet boots and coats! You'll get me skinned."

Jack's mother, however, had come through the door that led to the house. "Of course they can come in," she said. "What do you mean letting them stand about out here in the cold?

Come you on in, the lot of you." They went through, kicking off their boots while she berated her husband. "Can't you see that poor girl's half frozen?"

He chuckled. "Well you'll have a chance to warm her up. She's staying to have some dinner with us."

"So I should think," and she turned her back on him.

Mrs Smith was a small woman, rather stout, and she panted as she ushered them upstairs. "That old clock," she said, "he guards it like it was something human. Look at it, the way it stands there, getting in everyone's way like it owns the place."

And the clock did cramp the landing. Its top almost touched the low ceiling, and there was not enough room for them all to get close to it.

"I'll leave you," said Mrs Smith, "but Jack, don't you touch anything or your dad'll be on your tail."

"I don't have much chance," he said. "It's always locked."

In that case, Simon asked, why had he brought them up here?

"It was that drawing in the lid of the tool-box; it made me think of something." The dim light on the landing threw too many shadows so he fetched a torch from his bedroom and shone it through the glass front of the long case. Within it, the pendulum carved the air in

100

the swing it had kept up for more than a century. "Locked away," he said, "so no one can get to it."

"Someone must touch it," said Sophie. "It's been polished." The rod and brass weight shone golden.

"Once a year," said Jack. "My dad stops it for a few seconds and shines it up. Then he makes sure it's right by the church clock out there." Through the little window at the end of the landing they could see the tower.

"Now I get it!" Simon was excited. "There must be two clocks working together – just like the clock at the train station and the Railway Timepiece. Maybe the stars don't play such a large part, after all." He stood back, frowning as he gazed at the grandfather clock. "Does that mean that *this* is the Midwinter Watch?"

Jack shook his head. "No ... a watch is something you can put in your pocket."

"So why make all the fuss about this old clock?"

Sophie would not allow them to quarrel. "At least I can see the J and the S," she said. The rod and the weight were decorated with engravings. She could make out that the rod did form the long shaft of the letter J, and there was an elaborate S inscribed on the disc of the weight. But there was still something else on Jack's mind.

"The toolbox lid downstairs," he reminded her. "Do you remember what the writing said?"

She recalled the words. "They said *Jack Smith Keep Time Turning.*"

"No." Once more Jack shook his head. "Those letters don't stand for Jack Smith – they are separate: J and S, not JS together. They stand for Jack and Silas and they both keep time turning. It's not wrong at all."

Simon sniffed, unconvinced. "So what's the difference?"

Jack shone his torch on the pendulum. "That's the difference. Jack and Silas are swinging together ... and that's how they *keep time turning.* By being together."

He looked from one to the other. Their faces were blank.

He turned away and brought his beam to bear on the pendulum bob. "And that's it!" he said. "We have been looking at it all the time – that is the Midwinter Watch! It has to be."

"It doesn't look much like a watch to me." Simon peered at it. "There's no face."

"That's because it's old-fashioned," Jack insisted. "The face has a cover over it."

Sophie bent to examine it closer. He could be right. There was a rim. "And it's thick enough to be a watch," she said.

"There's one thing you've forgotten." Simon straightened. "If that is the Midwinter

Watch, it won't be of any use. Wasn't it supposed to have been kept going for more than a century without stopping? Don't tell me your father knows about it and has kept it wound up – and his father before him. That is ridiculous!"

He had to be right. Sophie glanced at Jack expecting to see cruel disappointment in his face. But his eyes still shone. "You've missed something," he said, and once more pointed the beam at the pendulum's long brass rod. "It's much thicker than it needs to be," he said. "Much too thick. There's enough room for another rod inside it."

Simon leant forward, suddenly interested. "You mean something inside the rod that turns each time it swings…"

"That's right." Jack was nodding vigorously. "And as it turns it could keep the watch wound up. And nobody has ever seen it because all the mechanism is sealed up."

"There's only one way to find out." Simon was keen to follow it up. "Open this glass door and take a closer look."

"I can't. My dad has the key and he won't let it out of his sight."

"Then tell him about it."

Jack heard Sophie catch her breath. Her mother was in danger, and Toby Heron believed the danger would get worse if too many people knew too much. But surely this had changed everything. "There's only one way to find out and still keep it to ourselves," he said. "I'll wait until everyone's asleep and then I'll try to get the key."

They had no choice, and they were on their way downstairs before Sophie realized there was still a problem. "How are you going to let us know when you get it?" she asked. "We are not going to have much time to do anything with it."

She was right. Jack's head drooped as he thought about it, but Simon's mind seemed to be on something else. "That's quite a powerful torch you've got," he said.

Jack shrugged, but Simon continued, "When you've got the Midwinter Watch you could signal to me."

"How can I? I can't see your house from here."

"No, but you can see that." Simon pointed through the landing window to where the church tower lifted above the rooftops. "And I can see it, too ... from my bedroom. You can shine your torch on the weathercock, and I'll come here when I see it."

"What about me?" said Sophie. "I can't see it from the gatehouse."

"Don't worry." Jack was leading the way downstairs. "We'll both come to fetch you."

CHRISTMAS EVE

Frozen snow crackled underfoot as they left the village and followed the road to the gate-house. The short afternoon was giving way to a starlight night but the sparkle that was everywhere around them was pitiless. With every breath that clouded the air Sophie yearned to turn back and shout to the whole village that her mother was out there somewhere in the snow, a prisoner. It had taken both Jack and Simon to convince her she must wait. The grandfather clock, with its secret, was their only hope.

"But Toby Heron has got to know what we are doing!" she said. "I'll have to tell him what to expect."

"Whatever that may be," said Simon. The biting cold was making him wonder what they were doing wandering in this white wasteland.

Jack would not share his doubts. "The

Midwinter Watch is there ... in the clock." His eyes were on Sophie. She was as pale and smooth as the Snow Queen; untouchable. "The Watch has got to be in the pendulum," he said. "All the signs say it is."

"Signs!" Simon shook his head and turned his face to the stars.

Sophie, in all her turmoil, knew they must not quarrel. "Toby Heron will know what to do," she said, and she quickened her pace when they came in sight of his muffled figure standing at the gateway to the drive. He was still no more than a black silhouette against the bars of the gates and she was about to break into a trot when she suddenly stopped. It was not Toby who stamped his feet and hunched his shoulders against the cold. It was Reg Boston, and he had seen her. He stood motionless, waiting for her.

"Where have you been?" His voice had no friendliness in it.

"I've been to the village." She hesitated. "That's all."

"Why weren't you at home? Your mother's been worried about you."

She was startled. "You mean she's here?"

"Of course she's here." He was suspicious. "What did you expect?"

"I don't know. I'll go and see her." She was moving past him when he put out an arm.

"She isn't in the house."

"Well, where is she? I want to see her!" Her anxiety was giving too much away, and it was Jack who grasped her hand and held her back.

"There's nothing to be alarmed about, Sophie." Boston smiled stiffly and changed his tone to calm her. "She's up at the Hall, waiting for you."

"You said she was worried about me ... why is she up there?"

Jack, squeezing her fingers until they hurt, spoke to the man. "She's with Toby Heron, isn't she?"

"You've got the idea, son." Boston, still smiling, raised one eyebrow at Sophie. "Toby's the man to comfort the ladies. They're both waiting for you."

Jack glanced at Sophie. She was calmer. "I'll come up to the Hall with you," he said.

"I'm afraid not, old boy." Boston stepped in front of him. "We're shutting up for the night." He began hauling the gates closed, shoving snow aside. Sophie released herself from Jack's grip.

"I'll be all right," she said softly, and he had to watch through the bars of the gate as she left him. She was very small alongside Reg Boston as they walked towards the darkened Hall.

"Don't worry about her, Jack," said Simon. "We'll see her tonight."

It was true, but it did not make him feel any

less of a coward. He had let her go without a fight.

Cousin Will beamed at her as if he was bringing good news. "I'm afraid your mother is not here at present, my dear." He moved away from the library fireplace. "But do come in and warm yourself."

Sophie ignored him and looked towards Toby Heron. "Where is she?" she asked. The pounding of her heart made her voice tremble.

"Oh dear, oh dear!" Cousin Will spoke as if he was comforting a little child. "There's nothing to worry about: I will allow Mr Heron to explain, and then he will do something for us." He looked towards Toby. "Isn't that so, cousin?"

Toby sat in one of the high-backed library chairs. He did not get to his feet. "I have made a promise, Sophie," he said. "You have heard me talk about the Midwinter Watch many times…" he nodded to encourage her to agree and show no surprise "… and these two gentlemen wish to get their hands on it, so they have persuaded Lucy to help them."

She remembered just in time to seem surprised. "Where is she? What are they doing?"

He told her, little by little, and she did not have to pretend to be afraid, but at the end, he drew a deep breath and said, "So now that I know you are safe, Sophie, I shall have to tell them everything I know – even though I tell them the Midwinter Watch does not exist." At that she drew in her breath so sharply that all three men turned towards her, and she froze.

"Sophie?" said Toby. He was worried, but he still did not get to his feet. "Are you all right?"

She nodded. He was going to tell the men about the secret room and the papers. And that was the one thing he must not do. Not yet. She and Jack and Simon needed time. Her mother would understand. Just a little time.

"If I help them," said Toby, "they have promised to free Lucy."

And Sophie acted. As Toby uttered her mother's name she flung herself across the room and into his arms.

"She's safe." Toby comforted her. "We shall soon see her."

Terror had driven away tears, but she allowed great sobs to heave her shoulders as she murmured into his ear, "We've found the Watch!" His arm clamped tight around her and he raised his voice in order to hide the words she was whispering. "Tell them nothing," she breathed. "Nothing!"

And then Reg Boston hauled her back and she could say no more.

Simon and Jack stood under the lamp in the village square. The bright loops of streamers in the windows of the Blacksmith's Arms almost hid the glitter of the bottles behind the bar, and further along the street the cottages spilled squares of light onto the snow as if a party was about to begin.

"It's Christmas," said Simon. The idea seemed to surprise him.

"It doesn't feel like it." Jack looked beyond the cottages at the silent, smooth hills over which the blue-black sky stooped with its breastplate of stars. Then a door opened and snow sparkled in the sudden light as a woman hurried to a neighbour, carrying something wrapped in bright paper. The neighbour let her in and the door closed behind her. The night was full of secrets. It was wrong to say it did not feel like Christmas; but he and Simon were no part of it.

Reg Boston dragged Sophie across the room and made her stand by the wall. He was still holding her back as he menaced Toby. "The papers," he said, "where are they!"

Toby played for time. He shifted in his chair and it was then that Sophie caught a glimpse of rusty chain at his wrist. He was manacled to the chair arm. "Sorry to be like this, Sophie," he said, "but Reg found these ancient handcuffs in the cellar and dearly wanted to play with them. I've told him they belong on his own wrist, not mine."

Boston twisted her shoulder until pain made her wince. "Where are the papers!"

Time had run out for Toby. He smiled. "I burned them," he said.

In Forge Cottage, Jack's mother pretended not to smile as she watched him cross to the door of the living-room. "There he go again," she said. "What you up to, climbing them stairs every few minutes?"

Jack protested. "I don't do it every few minutes." It happened only once every half-hour, but he couldn't say that.

"You're up to something," she said. "I seen you gazing out of that landing window more than once."

"Lookin' out for his girlfriend, I shouldn't wonder," said his father.

She laughed. "Just you be quiet. Leave the boy alone."

"Or else he's expecting to see Santa Claus."

"Give over, Dad." Jack had to think quickly to disguise what he was really doing. "I was only seeing if more snow was coming."

"Ain't this Christmas white enough for you, then, Jack?"

His mother drew in her breath. "There's lots of folk wish it weren't as white as this. They haven't been able to get in anything like the proper amount of food."

"And drink," her husband added.

"You make sure there's always enough o' that!"

"But you're right though, gal," he agreed. "There won't be that big party Toby Heron was planning up at the Hall." He shook his head. "Pity … I always liked that do."

"And think of the children. What if they don't get their presents?" She tutted and shook her head. They were still talking as Jack quietly opened the door and left them.

Upstairs, he crept into his parents' bedroom. His father, when he changed from his work-clothes, left his keys on the chest of drawers until next day. Jack took them, unlocked the case of the grandfather clock, and replaced them. He could do nothing more until the house was quiet.

At the landing window he sent a stab of his torch beam at the weathercock on the church tower, and waited a few seconds until it glinted once more in reply. He and Simon had agreed to check the signal every half-hour. It would help to keep them awake later in the night. And then, if nothing went wrong, he would send the Morse code signal for the letter W, meaning that he had the Watch.

The only sound in the library was Boston's soft footfall as he moved closer to Toby Heron. His face was set in a sickly rage and the knuckles of his fists were white. A footstool was in his way. He kicked it clear and as it rattled into the hearth his toe caught the cord of an electric light. He stooped and ripped at it. Sophie could not stifle a cry. She knew what would happen next, and she could do nothing to prevent it.

Boston hauled at the cord. It led under the bookshelves, and as he tugged at it the lamp in the hidden room fell with a crash. Boston gazed at the shelves and, as the secret began to dawn on him, Toby moaned and his head drooped. He had surrendered, and the sight of him as he meekly told the men how to open the shelves terrified her. He had given in, and she was helpless.

The men plunged into the workroom, but the instant they were out of sight Toby beckoned her. He seemed himself again, and she was moving towards him when Cousin Will reappeared and saw her. He shook his head. "I think not," he said, and advanced on Toby with Grandfather Silas's workshop notes in his hand. He thrust them under Toby's nose.

"I think these are what we have been seeking," he said. "All will be revealed before long ... unless you care to tell me here and now."

"I regret I can't help you, cousin." Toby's voice was stronger. "I am unable to fathom them out for myself."

"Very likely." Cousin Will showed his teeth

in a grin. "Let us see what a superior intelligence can do."

He sat at the table while Boston continued to ransack the workroom. Cousin Will worked quickly and seemed to have a plan in mind, for he rejected page after page until something caught his attention, and then he bent over to scrutinize a sheet of sketches near the end.

"What I am looking at is strangely illuminating," he murmured. "It appears that the village blacksmith, John Smith, did all the metalwork for your great-great-grandfather, including..." He broke off, turned to the last page, and once again thrust the sheaf in front of Toby. "Including this very interesting sketch of a grandfather clock."

Toby shut his mouth and said nothing, but Cousin Will was triumphant. "You may well knit your brows, my brave cousin, for I believe I have stumbled on the blacksmith's secret!"

He summoned Boston from the workshop. "The blacksmith will unlock the secret for us, Reg." His eyes rested on Sophie. "And I have the feeling that you know more than you pretend."

She held herself rigid. There was nothing more to be done. He knew everything.

"The blacksmith," he repeated. "He made the watches and he made the clocks, big and little ... little and big... Small enough and large

114

enough, in fact, for one to be within the other." He paused, enjoying the expression on her face. "But where, as the storyteller said, is the best place to hide a leaf? Why, in a forest, of course! So where is the best place to hide a watch? In a clock! So all we have to do now is to lay our hands on a rather large clock and I think we shall have solved our problem."

He turned to Boston. "A rather large clock, Reg. I wonder where that is to be found." He was taunting them, but Boston had already made up his mind and was moving away down the length of the library. A grandfather clock stood in the corner.

"Tell me, Toby." Cousin Will stooped over him. "Are we at our journey's end?"

Toby shook his head. "No. There's nothing in there." His voice was no more than a sigh, and Sophie's heart sank. Now, at last, he had completely given up.

Cousin Will turned to Boston. "Pay no attention! Tear its heart out!"

It was Boston's type of work. He yanked open the glass front of the grandfather clock, pulled out the pendulum and searched the case. He found nothing, so he lifted the glass-fronted hood from the face and dropped it on the floor. Even before it smashed he was feverishly exploring the clockwork.

"He won't find anything." Toby Heron's mumble was so indistinct that his cousin had to stoop to hear it. "I took out the Midwinter Watch long ago."

The grandfather clock crashed to the ground. "There's nothing!" Boston roared as he strode across the floor, pushed Cousin Will aside and grabbed the front of Toby Heron's shirt, twisting it under his chin. "Where is it!"

Toby, choking, managed to turn away from him. "I'm sorry, Sophie." He was gasping, barely able to speak. "I have to tell them."

"Leave the girl out of it!" Boston forced Toby to face him. "Where is the Midwinter Watch!"

"Her mother has it." Toby shut his eyes. "I gave it to Lucy Nelson!"

NIGHT JOURNEY

The church clock had struck eleven before Jack's mother came to bed, followed soon after by his father, and at half-past Jack had crept out of his room to make his signal to Simon. Now he was waiting until he was sure they were both asleep.

He had not undressed, and had not even lain on his bed for fear of drowsing. His clothes did not seem to fit him, he was uncomfortable in his armpits and crotch, and the night chilled his neck as he sat on the landing and waited. His head had drooped between his shoulders and his breathing had become long and gentle when a sound startled him and jerked him fully awake. He listened. His father had started to snore, and it was time to act.

Simon had a different problem. His parents never went to bed until long after midnight, so he would have to climb down from his bedroom window when Jack gave the signal. And Simon was terrified of heights; even lowering himself down a rope was too much for him.

He opened his bedroom door and listened. They were watching a late-night Christmas movie and were certain to be awake when he had to leave. Simon shut the door and crossed his room. He had made his preparations.

A length of string was tied to his window catch and led outside. He opened the window and began pulling it in. It was secured to the end of a coil of washing line which he began to haul in. It was frozen and clumsy to handle and he doubted that even Jack would have expected him to climb down it. But he had something else in mind, and he was ready for the signal whenever it came.

Jack had also prepared himself. During the day he had taken what he thought he might need from the clockmaker's toolbox, and he had a slim bundle of tools wrapped in a cloth so they would not rattle.

The landing was dark but he dared not switch on the light. He moved in his socks towards the grandfather clock before he switched on his torch, shielding the beam with his hand. The glass-fronted door swung smoothly but he had not reckoned how loudly the beat of the old clock would echo once its case was open.

He held his breath, ready to close the door on the sound and slither out of sight as fast as he could if his parents should stir. But his father's snore measured itself in harmony with the old clock's steady tick.

He let his beam follow the swing of the pendulum. For more than a century the Smiths of Lott's Bend had guarded it and breathed life into it, but now he was going to bring that to an end. The dark landing creaked with the ghosts of dead blacksmiths and their heavy hands slowed his arm as he reached for the swinging disc and his fingers closed over it. A last tick, and then silence. The return beat was choked off, and in that instant his parents' room fell deadly still. His father's breathing had stopped, and Jack's own breath caught in his throat until, with a choked shudder, his father resumed measuring out the night. And Jack laughed.

He was still giggling as he tried to unhook the pendulum bob. It did not lift off. He held the shaft and tried to disengage the bob. It would not lift or permit itself to be twisted. He crouched, and with his shoulders half within the case, examined the brass disc. There was no screw that could be undone or nut that he could turn with the tools. The bob was all of a piece with the pendulum shaft and would not budge.

He sat back on his heels. The engraved initials of Jack and Silas were very clear. The very long upright of the letter J ran the whole length of the brass rod, and the hook of the J at the bottom ran around the edge of the disc and enclosed the elaborate S in many flourishes. It was all so much out of proportion it was hardly surprising nobody had noticed it.

As he pondered, his eyes followed the engraved marks down the shaft to where they smoothly joined the brass disc. No. It wasn't as smooth a join as it seemed; the engraver had not been quite accurate. He frowned. He was wasting time. He picked a screwdriver from his roll of tools and bent closer. He would lever the bob free of the pendulum even if he had to destroy it.

His breath misted the shining face of the disc, and it was then that he saw what he had been looking for. It was there, at the point where the engraving was not perfect. The lines cut into the brass face did not join up because they had to cross a hairline crack, and at some time in the last hundred years the face of the disc had turned by the tiniest fraction.

Jack put down his screwdriver, and with one hand held the back of the pendulum while he grasped the face of the disc as if he was unscrewing the top of a jar. There was the slight resistance of something that had not budged for many years, but then the disc turned. It was not even stiff. The thread of the screw face had been so finely machined that it came off without any forcing, and behind it, nested in solid brass, was the Midwinter Watch. It was a fat golden egg and all he could see of its face was the gleam of blue enamel through a small circular window at the centre of its cover. Enough of its hands was visible through the little window for him to tell that it was keeping perfect time.

He gripped it, but had to fumble to free it from its connection with the grandfather clock whose swinging pendulum had kept it alive in the dark for generations. He looked at it closely. There was a stud at its rim which could be pressed to open the cover. When it sprang open in Heron Hall they would know if old Silas's words were true. He held it to his ear. Its tick was a tiny heartbeat.

He had the Midwinter Watch in his hands and now he realized he had not given a thought to how he would protect it. He wrapped it in the yellow duster from his tools and buttoned it into his shirt pocket. It was heavy and made an uncomfortable bulge, but it was safe. He hid the tools in the base of the grandfather clock, screwed the face of the pendulum bob back into place and set it swinging. Its beat seemed less certain, and Jack found that he was trembling as he went to the end of the landing and aimed his torch at the weathercock.

His first stab missed its mark and fell on the parapet of the church tower. He steadied his hand against the window ledge and paused as he drew a deep breath. It was then that he thought he saw a movement at the tower's top. The night held everything in its iron fingers yet his eye had caught a flicker of something that stirred against the white of the snow piled there. He gazed for a long moment but saw nothing more. Perhaps an owl had launched itself into the icy air. He guided his beam to the tip of the spire and held it steady. The golden cockerel, its comb capped in white, glinted above the rooftops. He switched off.

There was no reply. The cockerel stood against the stars, dark and lonely. Simon was asleep, and their plan was about to go wrong. He dipped his head, wondering what to do next, when suddenly the cockerel's golden feathers seemed to shake themselves. It glowed. Simon was awake.

And now to give him the signal they had agreed when the Midwinter Watch was found. Jack's finger tapped out the code for W, a dot and two long dashes, and Simon's reply came so swiftly it was as though they were shouting to each other over the sleeping village.

In his bedroom Simon put down his torch. It was time to act. Like Jack he was already dressed for the night, and he opened his window to haul at the rope.

His mother and father heard a noise outside but thought it was no more than snow sliding from a roof and turned back to the television screen. If they had gone to the window and pushed back the curtain they would have seen a ladder raise itself from the snow and stand upright on its own two feet for a moment before it lost balance and began to fall towards the house.

Simon leant out of the window as the ladder tilted towards him. He grasped the rungs and eased it gently into place so that it did not clatter against the wall. Then, shivering more with anxiety than from the cold, he got his legs over the sill and began to climb down.

Jack lingered at the landing window. Once again his eye had caught a movement behind the parapet of the church tower. At this distance it was no more than a vague shadow against the snow, but it was larger than an owl. He shook his head; it was time to go, and he was imagining things. But just before he turned away he aimed his torch for the last time at the tower.

"I'm being stupid," he murmured, "there's nothing there." He was wasting time but he let his beam slide along the parapet towards the little pinnacle at the corner. It did not get there. It had touched on something else. Someone stood there; alone on the church tower, in the freezing night.

Jack's clenched hand refused to release the button. The light played on the lonely figure in its slate-grey clothes, and his eyes focused on the pale blur of its face until he could make out its haggard features. It was the face that had looked down on him when he sprawled in the snow at the foot of the churchyard wall. The Starveling Boy gazed at him again.

Jack's breath fluttered in his throat, and his hand trembled as the Boy raised both hands high and waved his arms, signalling across the rooftops, as if he and Jack were two of a kind, a pair of ghosts together.

Jack let out his breath in a little cry that sounded more like a sob, his light went out, and he stumbled downstairs careless of what sound he made and stood gasping in the kitchen. He listened, struggling to calm the leaping of his heart. The house was quiet, and after a while he pulled on his boots. No matter what else was out there, Simon was waiting for him.

HUNTING
THE WATCH

It was a lie, and Toby Heron repeated it. "Lucy Nelson has the Midwinter Watch," he said, and the handcuffs on his wrist rattled as he turned to face Sophie. "I gave it to your mother, Sophie. I'm sorry." She was startled. Of the four people in the room only she herself had any idea of where the Watch could be. Yet Toby kept his eyes on her and she could tell he was pleading with her not to contradict him. "I gave it to her," he said. "I thought I could get away with it."

"Let's have a look at you." Reg Boston put his face close to Toby's. "Are you being honest with me, old friend?"

"I have nothing to gain," said Toby. "You've got the better of me."

Their eyes locked, and after a while a slow, satisfied smile creased Boston's face. "You always were a truthful little boy." He held

Toby's head between his thick hands. "A truthful, fat little boy, isn't that so, chubby cheeks?" He pressed his hands so that Toby's face was distorted. "And you know when you're beaten. We have the woman, so we have the Watch. Both conveniently together." He laughed. "I just hope that Watch is keeping her warm in Scalybank Halt. She'll be needing it."

"One moment." Cousin Will came closer and looked down on Toby. "I am not so trusting as my friend Reg," he said. "Mrs Nelson could still be a danger to us … the Midwinter Watch is a powerful instrument."

Toby shook his head free. "You have no need to worry." He closed his eyes and sighed. "She does not know what it is, and has no idea what it can do. How could she find out? I have had no time to tell her, I swear to that."

It was the first true thing he had said, and suddenly Sophie knew he was giving her a message. He was once again playing for time. It was all he could do. If only she could tell him what she knew.

Boston had taken a slip of paper from his wallet. "Very useful, this." He waved it at Toby, taunting him. "It's the old boy's timetable. We'll be catching the midnight mail."

"And you come with us." Cousin Will stooped to unlock the handcuffs and shackle

126

Toby's hands behind his back. "And the girl." He gripped the hood of Sophie's coat and held on to it as they left.

The cold reached in to pinch Jack's ears as he opened the door. In the dimness of the lane the snow was a dull white and he was reluctant to step out into the night where the Starveling Boy roamed. He had one foot on the step when he saw a movement at the lane's end, and he drew back. He watched, and the movement came again, but this time with a muffled cough and the sound of a shuffling footstep. Simon was waiting for him.

In a corner of the square they huddled together and looked at the Watch. "Is it gold?" Simon held it so that the street light fell on the gleaming watchcase with the small window that showed its face. "How does it work?" He looked up and saw that Jack was gazing towards the church tower. "Is something wrong?"

"I'm not sure." No figure waved from the parapet. How could he tell Simon that he had seen a ghost? Once before he had said nothing, but now he began to hint at it. "There's something going on," he said, "but I don't know what it is."

Simon turned to where Jack was gazing, and drew in his breath sharply. "You're right!" he said. "What the devil's that?"

The parapet was bare. "I can see nothing!"

"There!" Simon was pointing beyond the tower at something in the distance.

A light sparkled in the snow. A pretty sight on Christmas eve. Two lights. And then he saw what it was. The beams of a car's headlamps played on the snow banked at the roadside as it rocked and swayed over the frozen ruts. It was coming from the Hall.

"Toby Heron." Jack was moving out to meet it when Simon pulled him into the doorway of the store. "How do we know it's him?" he said.

The headlights swept the square. Only the windscreen was free of ice and they could not make out the driver nor who sat beside him. And in the back seat were the vague outlines of two other figures.

Jack gripped the Watch in his pocket. He had been in danger of letting it fall into the wrong hands.

Sophie's chance had gone. The square was the only place where it would have made sense to cry out and make a disturbance, anything to delay them, but Boston's heavy hand had reached out and clamped her shoulder. Now the square was behind them and the houses had petered out.

Her hopes rose for a moment when Cousin Will steered into Station Lane and the car slithered and the wheels spun. But then it edged forward between the trees where the snow was less deep and they were in the station yard far out of earshot of anyone in the village.

"Out!" Boston stood by the door and watched as she stepped down, but he had no need to fear she would break away; the snow was too deep for her to run. Toby Heron, unable to balance properly, would have fallen if Cousin Will had not supported him. "No tricks, my friend. We are cutting it rather fine and I don't suppose you would want to miss seeing the lady."

Toby turned away from him. "I'm sorry, Sophie, but he's right. At least we'll be seeing your mother soon – and that's all that matters."

An idea crossed her mind. "I knew all along she had the Midwinter Watch," she said.

"You did?" Even in the faint snowlight she could see surprise on his face.

"She showed it to me," said Sophie. He would know it was a blatant lie. "We know where you found it. We know the place – we know."

His eyes searched her. "You know?"

Boston cut across them. "No more gab," he said, and hauled her up the steps to the station platform.

From somewhere in the distance a whistle

echoed across the lonely snow and from the cutting clouds of steam swelled up into the stars as the train panted out of the night and came rumbling and hissing to a stop alongside the platform.

THE ICY HAND

The car had no sooner passed the shop doorway than Simon and Jack began to follow. All they had been able to make out was that one of the occupants was smaller than the rest. "Sophie," said Jack, and they ran after it down the centre of the road. Its headlights raked sideways into Station Lane, and they paused at the corner, panting. There were no lights. Somewhere ahead of them the car had stopped.

Simon gasped through a haze of breath. "I can't hear a train."

"We've got to get to her!" Jack led the way. "She must be with Toby Heron."

"And who else?" muttered Simon, but Jack wasn't listening. He had heard the rumble of wheels on the line.

They ran, staggering in the ruts, and stumbled into the station yard just as steam and smoke came billowing down over the station roof. Even before they reached the car they knew it was empty and they ran for the station steps. Jack slipped on the ice and fell just as a figure swinging a lamp turned from the platform and came towards him. They were in plain view of the man but he appeared not to notice, and he put down the lamp, stamped snow from his feet, went into the ticket office and slammed the door.

"It's a porter!" Simon whispered, and they were about to creep forward when the flame of the lamp he had left by the door dwindled and went out, and the lamp vanished. They ran through to the platform, but the train had already been swallowed by the swirling snow.

Jack punched his hand. He was useless. They had got away, Sophie was with them, and he had done nothing.

Reg Boston was still on his feet brushing snow from his shoulders as the train gathered speed. Sophie glanced under his arm at Toby in the far corner of the compartment and he gave her a rueful smile as the wheels squealed into the sharp curve just outside the station and the carriage rocked. Boston had to cling to the luggage rack, and for the split second she was out of his sight Sophie reached for the door handle.

"No!" Toby's bellow came at the instant a

sudden draught from the door made Boston swing his head. They were both too late.

Sophie did no more than turn the handle. She had no control over what happened next. The door, caught in the rush of air, swung open of its own accord, lifted her from her seat and flung her out.

The handle was ripped from her fingers and she flew out into the huge hollow of the night. This was the end. She would hit something. She spread her arms and screwed up her face for the cruel impact that was rushing at her.

She hit. Her sleeves scooped snow and sent up a fountain that bit her face and blinded her. Her bones jarred and her lungs emptied as a great cold fist closed over her and held her tight.

She ceased to move. She drew in her breath. It groaned in her throat and she was certain she must be injured. She tried to push herself upright and felt no pain, but a weight of snow pressed on her and held her still. She was buried deep in a snowdrift. She began to struggle, and found she could do no more than wriggle her fingers. Even her arms were fixed. She was trapped in stony darkness and panic leaped inside her.

She was choking, writhing uselessly, when the fingers of one hand felt the snow give slightly. She scratched feverishly at it, but suddenly her fingers were locked in ice. Her panic

133

flared again, and with it came pain. The ice that clamped her hand began to move, and first her elbow and then her shoulder felt the strain as she was dragged through the press of snow and out into the night.

The grip on her fingers eased and fell away. Trembling and staggering, she got to her feet. She was gasping her thanks as she rubbed the caked snow from her eyes so that she could see her helper. A tree spilled snow from an over-burdened branch, and for a moment seemed to take shape, but her eyes were misted and it vanished. The moon's calm light showed the railway line stretching away into the distance, and it was deserted. She was alone.

On the station platform Jack and Simon saw the train disappear around the bend and turned away. They were passing the ticket office when Simon glanced along the empty track and stopped. "There's someone moving," he muttered. A dark figure showed against the snow.

"Two people," said Jack, but then it was only one. A girl stood in the centre of the track. Sophie.

She saw him jump from the platform and run towards her. Simon was with him. No one was near her but her wrist still felt the pressure of the icy fingers that had hauled her free. She looked back and the silent night seemed to be stealthily closing in on her, but she saw nothing. She was still gazing down the track when the boys came level.

"I jumped," she said, and struggled to stop herself shuddering as she told them what had happened. "I was buried ... but someone helped me out."

Simon listened and looked. "I see where you fell," he said, "and there's a bush just under the snow." Some spindly branches showed above the surface. "Those are the fingers you felt."

She hardly heard him. Other things crowded her mind.

"The Midwinter Watch!" She clutched at Jack's arm. "Did you find it?" He was still taking it out of his pocket when her words came tumbling over each other. "They think my mother's got it ... Toby told them ... what will they do when they find out!"

Jack had no choice. The Midwinter Watch was in his hand. As long as he had it they could bargain. "We've got to get to them," he said.

"But how?" Scalybank Halt was away down the line, out of sight. "What do we do?"

"It's obvious." Their heads jerked towards Simon. "But we've got to be quick." He pointed along the track. "There's no snow on the track and it's not far to Scalybank."

They began to run, keeping to the sleepers, trying not to stumble.

"The train swept it clear," said Jack. He should have thought of that himself.

"No," said Simon. "The train came through in a different time to ours when there wasn't so much snow. We are still in that time." He knew now that when the train was running they were in the past; and the past began to fade into the present once the train had gone by. He remembered the porter's oil lamp that dwindled and vanished after the train left the station. "We are still in the past," he panted, "but it won't last long. When it's gone the track fills up with snow again." He had watched it happen when the train went through before. "A few minutes. That's all we've got."

Once they had rounded the bend, the line was on a long level stretch cut into the side of the hill. The slope rose above them on one side of the track and fell sharply away on the other. Scalybank Halt was no more than a shack and they searched for it as they ran, but already, above the pounding of their hearts, they heard a sound like muffled thunder creeping up on them from behind.

Somewhere ahead was the Halt. They could see only trees and shadows. Perhaps it no longer existed. And then Jack saw a faint spark of red.

"Tail lamp," he gasped. It was not moving. The train was at the Halt, and he had the

Watch. Everything depended on him. He surged ahead, forcing his legs to pump faster.

His eyesight was blurred, but now he could make out the rear of the train and the flicker of the flame in the oil lamp. And there was the hut beside the track with the land sloping steeply away beneath it.

There was still time. There had to be time.

But then, like a thin shriek of laughter, the engine whistle bit into the night and the train began to roll. It gathered speed and its lamp dwindled, but the rumble of wheels remained … except that now the sound seemed to be running them down from behind. He glanced back and saw a dancing wall of white foam filling up the line, catching up on Sophie and Simon.

He stopped and turned. "Run!" he yelled. "Run!"

They saw what was happening but could sprint no faster. The white powder was at their heels and they plunged on until a surge caught them behind their knees and their legs were clamped.

Jack began to run back to haul them free but within a few paces the tide was around his own ankles and brought him down. He saw Sophie buried up to her waist and he was floundering towards her on all fours when the rumble of the avalanche died in a smothered sigh and powdered snow came sifting down over his head and shoulders.

And then, when there should have been silence, there was the sound of voices. He was crouching, held fast, and all he could do was to blink snow from his eyes.

Two figures were coming towards him, thrusting a passage through the edges of the drift, and one of them spoke.

"So there you are, Master Jack Smith." Cousin Will looked down on him. "Well met by moonlight."

He left it to Reg Boston to grab Jack by the shoulders and hoist him upright. Jack fought, but he had no chance. Boston knew what to look for. He pinned Jack's arms behind his back and searched his pockets until his fingers closed over the Midwinter Watch.

THE SNOW TUNNEL

Half choked by snow, Sophie and Simon were dragged free and herded with Jack into the hut.

"Sophie!" Her mother's face was pinched by the cold hours she had spent alone, and the sight of Sophie alarmed her. "Are you hurt?" She was hugging her and brushing snow from Sophie's hair. "Why have they brought you here?"

"Mother and daughter reunited." The light of the single candle deepened the creases of Cousin Will's face. "Isn't that a touching sight, Reg? And to think you and I were responsible for bringing them together…"

Boston's broad shoulders almost filled the hut's doorway. He held up a hand in which the Midwinter Watch gleamed. "Thank you for this, Toby. It's been a great pleasure, but I am afraid it's time to go."

The guttering candle-end tinged Cousin Will's smile with yellow. "We have a train to catch."

Toby Heron tugged at his wrist which was manacled to a shelf bracket. "You can't leave us like this!" His voice was thick with anger. "If you don't care about me – think of the others. They will never be found until it's too late. They will freeze!"

"Oh." Cousin Will was primly surprised. "We can't have that, can we? I shall leave the key." He turned and threw it out into the snow.

"Happy Christmas to you all!" Boston slammed the door behind him and they heard something heavy dragged along the boards and wedged against it.

Toby heaved at the bracket but only succeeded in sending the candle tumbling to the floor where it went out. And at the same moment they heard a train arriving.

"The window!" Jack shouted. It was boarded up but one of the slats was rotten. He hauled at it and it split. Through the gap he saw a carriage begin to move. It was heading back to Lott's Bend. If they could get out they could run down the track for help before the snow closed in again. But the slats were nailed fast and the gap was too small.

Toby Heron grunted, heaving with all his weight on the bracket. It came down and brought the shelf with it. Together they used it as a battering ram. Glass crashed and fell out, but the window bars were solid, and time was running out. Sophie pushed herself forward.

"I can get through," she said, and they could not stop her. She felt glass tear at her sleeve, but she was through.

Jack watched through the gap. She ran two paces and stopped. "Run, Sophie! Run!" He shouted.

She did not seem to hear. He shouted again. She remained where she was, unable to move. Jack could not see what it was that prevented her.

The Starveling Boy stood at the edge of the platform. He was close enough for her to see the sunken cheeks of his young face that seemed so old, and the terrible thinness that made his knees and ankles too large for his frail body. His eyes were no more than ghastly shadows in his gaunt face, but he was not a threat. He spread his hands as if he wanted her to stand still.

She heard Jack clamber through the window just as the snow plunged from the hillside to cover the track, but her eyes remained on the Boy. He pointed at something at his feet and almost immediately faded and vanished. All Jack saw was that she walked a few paces and stooped. When she straightened she had the key to the manacles. "It was the Boy," she said. "He showed me."

Simon had scrambled out and together they shifted the old railway sleeper that Boston had wedged against the door. She handed the key to Simon to free Toby and he went inside, leaving them alone on the platform.

The ground fell away sharply from where they stood, and they could see Lott's Bend far below, sinking into the rising tide of darkness that flooded the valley as the moon went down behind the hills. The snow was a bottomless quicksand that would suck them down. The village was out of reach.

They were turning away when a whisper made them pause. It could only be the last of the snow sifting down across the line, and Jack looked towards where the powder should have been settling. There was no movement, but the whisper continued. He saw nothing until Sophie touched his arm.

Beyond the edge of the platform the Starveling Boy stood on the slope. His mouth was opening and closing as though he spoke, but all that reached them was the thin hiss of a freezing breeze that trembled the uppermost twigs of the bushes buried on the hillside. And the Boy beckoned them towards the slope.

Sophie began to move, but Jack held her back. "You can't," he said. "It's too dangerous." She shook him free and stepped from the platform on to the slope. It was the place where the snow was deepest. He saw her feet sink in, and as they did so a great shelf of snow broke free and carried her away. He lunged but was too late. The Starveling Boy had betrayed them.

In the hut they heard Jack's shout and ran to his side. They saw Sophie outlined against the white, helplessly carried by the avalanche which carved a hollow before it piled up against a line of bushes and paused there before its weight sent it plunging away out of sight in a diminishing roar. They stood with the bitter air biting their throats as their eyes feverishly searched, but she had gone. All that remained was a black wall of exposed bushes.

And then, on the stripped slope, a figure moved and beckoned. Sophie's mother darted forward, but Jack put out a hand to hold her back. It was not Sophie. It was the Starveling Boy. Jack could see the fluttering rags luring them into more danger, but as they watched they heard a voice calling to them, clear on the air.

"It's Sophie!" Lucy Nelson would not be held back and Jack went with her. The Boy disappeared against the dark bushes, but as they slithered down the slope in the wake of the avalanche, Sophie's voice continued to call. Jack caught sight of her where the Boy had vanished.

"There's a way through!" she cried. "He

showed me."

They came level with her, panting. Lucy Nelson was in a daze. "Who showed you?" she asked, but the only answer Sophie gave was to turn and point.

Bushes that still bore the weight of snow had bent over and made a cave. "Look," said Sophie, "it goes further – it's a tunnel. Under the snow. He wants us to follow."

"Who does?" Her mother could not see what was there.

A grey shape stood in the blackness of the entrance. Sophie tugged at Jack and they made their way through the frozen grass towards it. The others followed.

It was like walking through the heart of a wave. The snow arched overhead and in patches it was thin enough for the moon to cast a ghostly light on the crooked track. They had to walk in single file, sometimes tripping over the spindly black branches that curved up like ribs to support the roof, and after a while they left Toby Heron and Lucy Nelson far enough behind to tell Simon about the Starveling Boy.

He glanced back. "Why didn't you say anything to them?"

"They'd be just like you," said Sophie, "they wouldn't believe it."

Jack was pressing ahead. Why didn't Simon just shut up?

"They'd believe you," said Simon. "They're crazy enough."

Sophie glanced back to see her mother stumble and Toby Heron put his arm around her. He kept it there.

"See what I mean?" said Simon.

Sophie yanked at a branch and snow smothered his head.

"Nice one," said Jack, and they went forward laughing.

The tunnel was crooked and at times low and narrow so the going was difficult and they lost track of where they were. Talking became too much of an effort, and they went tunnelling through the night not knowing where they may emerge. And suddenly Jack, who was leading, could go no further.

"Snow block," he said. "We've reached the end."

They were getting their breath back when Toby caught up. He seemed happy, and it was catching. "Stand aside," he said. "This is a job for the heavy brigade."

"You can say that again," said Simon, and Jack laughed.

Toby turned to Sophie. "If one of these two is your boyfriend," he said, "hit him."

She hit Simon. "So he's the chosen one?" said Toby.

"Not necessarily," said Sophie, and hit Jack.

"Now you've made them both happy," said

Toby, and he and Lucy Nelson laughed together. It was the strangest place to be laughing, but Toby said, "Adds a bit of spice," and thrust his bulk against the snow wall. The last barrier collapsed, but he did not rush into the open. He stood stock-still and whispered, "Listen!"

Jack pushed forward. He recognized where they were. They had broken through into the station yard, and the sound that had brought Toby to a standstill was the hiss and breathing of an engine.

"I don't understand this," Simon whispered. "The train should have gone through long ago. Why is it still at the station?"

Jack hushed him, and pointed. Just beyond the ticket office they could see one of the carriages, and the dim light from its window showed a shadowy figure occupied with something on the platform. "They're busy unloading the goods van," he muttered, and they heard the muffled slither of a heavy object being dragged along.

But Toby had seen something else. His car stood in the yard, and it was empty. "Now's our chance, Jack!" he said, and before anyone could hold him back he went plunging across the yard. The car was unlocked, and he turned with the ignition key in his hand. "Very careless," he said, and beckoned to the others.

They spilled out from the tunnel and were

crossing the yard when Jack saw the danger. Cousin Will was standing on the platform in the light of the carriage window. His attention was on something that was taking place further down the platform, but at that moment he turned his head and gazed towards the station yard. He saw them. His head jerked in surprise, and then Reg Boston was at his side.

Jack shouted, and across the yard Toby saw what was happening. He did not hesitate. He charged. Boston began to come forward to meet him but had taken no more than half a pace when Cousin Will spun him around and both of them moved quickly out of sight.

Jack and Toby leapt up the steps together, but they were too late. A carriage door slammed, a roar of steam made the wheels skid on icy rails before they gripped and with a shudder the train moved out. They ran onto an empty platform to see the tail lamp dimming behind a curtain of snow.

Toby laughed as he heaved to regain his breath. "Gone!" he panted. "Run away! They didn't dare tackle us all together. We've seen 'em off!"

"Not quite." Simon had not been far behind. He had, as usual, been thinking. "Nobody saw them get on the train," he said. "They could still be here."

"He's right!" Toby snatched his torch and marched to the ticket office. It was locked, but the torch beam showed it was empty. So was the waiting room. Only the parcels office remained. Its door was ajar. He pushed it. It swung open and his light swept the room. Shadows, but no movement.

"Empty," said Simon, but he was mistaken. There was a stack of boxes and parcels in the middle of the floor. They went towards it cautiously, but there was no one lurking there. The stack seemed like ordinary baggage until they went closer.

"So this is what they were unloading," said Toby. The packages were not dusty and neglected, as they should have been, and at least one of them was a large, square wickerwork basket. "An old hamper," he said, "except that it looks brand new. And look at this – when did you last see a crate tied up with rope in this way? And this brown paper parcel all done up with string and sealing wax – it all looks like something in the dim and distant past."

He was puffing around, lifting one thing after another and showing them to Sophie's mother. "My great-great-grandfather would have known about stuff like this," he said.

"I should think he would." Lucy Nelson was reading a label on one of the parcels. "It's addressed to him."

Toby threw back his head and roared at the ceiling. "That's it! It all belongs to old Silas

Heron – he ordered it!" He stamped around looking at labels. "All his! Grandfather Silas was the one who started it all. He gave the first big Christmas party and all of this must be the stuff he sent for!"

"There's so much of it!" said Sophie. "It's no wonder it took so long to unload."

"And my cousin stayed to see what it was." Toby chuckled. "He thought it might be something he could steal!"

Jack glanced at Simon and saw that the same uncomfortable thought had occurred to both of them. "They still have the Midwinter Watch," he said. "They'll be back."

"And so shall we." Toby bustled them towards the door. "We can't let all these crates and parcels go to waste." They crossed the yard. "Snowing again," he said, "so we'll know if they come back. There'll be footprints in Station Lane."

"We shall have to keep an eye on the station all day to see when a train brings them back." Simon had doubts. "That'll be awkward – it's Christmas."

"So it is!" Toby beamed at Lucy Nelson. "So let's not bother our heads about the Midwinter Watch just for the present – we'll have to prepare a feast at Heron Hall tonight that no one will ever forget!"

They drove off, and as their headlights left Station Lane in darkness the door of the ticket office opened. "Let them return and search as much as they please," said Cousin Will. "We shall not be here."

He and Reg Boston kept to the ruts as they walked towards the village.

PARTY? WHAT PARTY?

Simon's first mistake was to yawn too much at breakfast. It made his mother suspicious.

"This is not like you on Christmas morning," she said. "You usually have us up before dawn, but today I could hardly wake you and now you look as though you have been up all night."

"I have," he said dozily. "I climbed out of my window at midnight and took a walk along the railway line."

His father laughed at this, as Simon knew he would, but his mother was not put off so easily. "And you haven't even opened all your presents. That's not like you at all."

"Give the boy a break," said his father. "He's not a little kid any more, are you, Simon?"

Embarrassing. It prompted Simon to make his second mistake. "Got to get my rest up," he said, "for the party tonight."

"Party? What party?" They both wanted to know.

"Ah." Simon was suddenly wide awake. "Didn't you know?"

They shook their heads.

"I thought everyone knew. It's Toby Heron – in spite of the snow and everything he's decided he can give a big party after all, and he's inviting everyone. The whole village."

"Since when?" His father was sceptical. "I've heard nothing about it."

"Last night," he blurted out, and shut his eyes.

"Dreamer," said his mother. "Where does he think he's going to get all the food? Nobody in Lott's Bend has anything like as much as they're used to."

Honesty was his only get-out. "He's found a whole lot of stuff his great-great-grandfather ordered and never got round to using."

"Turkeys?" she said. "Christmas puddings?"

"I expect so."

His mother and father looked at each other and sighed.

Things were even more awkward for Jack. The grandfather clock had stopped and his father stood on the landing talking to it.

"All these years," he said sadly, "and you've

been quite contented, standing up here with a smile on your face every time I look at you. What's gone wrong, old girl?"

"Old boy," said Jack, "he's a grandfather." It was the best he could do, but he winced.

His mother came up the stairs. "You can soon put that old clock right," she said. "What bothers me is that son o' yours – I had to wake him up this morning. Christmas morning ... and him fast asleep!"

"I'm pretty sure I heard him moving about in the night, Mother." Jack drew in his breath, but his father winked at him. "So I reckon he's had a look in his stocking already."

Jack smiled, but his heart wasn't in it. His father would have given anything to have seen the Midwinter Watch, but he had taken it away in the middle of the night and lost it.

"I've got something else on my mind." His mother's eyes were on him, and she was worried. It was his clothes. He had come indoors in the night too tired to brush away all the snow, and now she suspected something.

"I was late getting in yesterday," he said weakly.

"I know you was." She seemed to be only partly satisfied. "But it weren't only that. What about that girl? That's who I'm thinking of."

"What girl?"

"You silly hap'orth." She was laughing at

him. "I'm talking about Sophie – you know Sophie, don't you?"

"He knows, all right," said his father. "He's blushing."

"You keep out o' this, John Smith. I ain't talking of anything like that, I'm thinking of that poor girl and her mother not in their own home at Christmas." She hushed her husband. "I know, I know they're with that man Boston, but from what you tell me he always likes to spend his Christmas down the pub, so I was thinking the two women might like to come and have Christmas dinner with us."

Jack opened his mouth, then shut it. He couldn't tell her of Toby Heron's party.

"So what you can do this morning," she told him, "is trot along and tell her mother that they're both very welcome."

And he had been wondering how he was going to get out of the house to talk to the others on Christmas morning without making everyone suspicious.

"Just look at him go," said his father as Jack began to pull on his boots. "I wonder what the attraction is."

There was a break in the weather, the sky was clear and the hills were as bright as china under the sun. They were polished by a cold wind that lifted a dust of snow to sting Jack's eyes as he stood just within the gateway of

Heron Hall and examined the gatehouse. It looked deserted and even footprints near the door had been smoothed by the sifting snow, but his mind nagged at the thought that Boston and Cousin Will might have returned while he slept; they could be watching him from the dark rooms behind the blank windows. And Sophie could be in danger again. He was still hesitating when a sound from the direction of the Hall jerked his head around. Reg Boston's pick-up was lurching down the drive.

He made an attempt to hide behind the gatepost, but he had been spotted. He was turning to make a run for it when a girl's voice called his name. Sophie was leaning out of the cab window. "Happy Christmas!" Her mother was with her and Toby Heron was driving.

"You didn't think we'd still be there, did you?" Sophie was laughing, and he felt foolish. "We are staying up at the Hall."

"Oh," he said.

"It's lovely!" She had woken in a bedroom larger than any she had ever seen.

"That's good."

"Smile, then."

He tried, but now he could not ask her to have Christmas dinner at Forge Cottage.

"Hey, Jack!" Toby Heron put his head out of the driver's window. "I was coming to see you. We've got a lot to talk about, you and me." Jack went to him. "Sophie's told me how you figured out how to find the Midwinter Watch. So what's it like? How do you think you make it work?"

Now that he did not have it in his hand Jack was unsure. "I didn't have much chance to look at it," he said, "but I know there's a stud on the rim and you must press that to open it." He remembered what Grandfather Silas had written: everything would be put to the test "when my Watch next opens." That had to be it. "All you have to do is open it," he told Toby. "You press the stud, the cover flies open, and then the past comes back ... if you are in the proper place."

"And we know where that is," said Toby.

"But they have it, and we haven't."

"Can't be helped." Toby had an elbow on the window ledge, his hat on the back of his head and a grin on his face as if everything was going his way. "At least we got the girls out of a spot of bother. That's what matters."

Odd to think of Sophie's mother as a girl. Jack glanced at her. She and Sophie were talking to each other just as if they were the same age. And even if he hadn't actually had to rescue Sophie in the night, as Toby seemed to think, he didn't mind if people thought so.

"First things first," said Toby. "We need your help down at the station, picking up all that stuff. Can you get that clever friend of yours to give us a hand on Christmas Day without rousing the populace and giving all our secrets away?"

"I'll say I've come about your party up at the Hall, and then they'll let him come out to help us spread the word that there's going to be a feast."

"Cunning," said Toby. "Quite brilliant."

It was a slithery ride in the back of the pick-up, and even worse in Station Lane but Simon had joined them without too many questions from his parents and when the truck pulled up in the station yard they were certain that no one knew where they were or what was happening. "And that's how we've got to keep it," said Toby. "Just we five together. If we start trying to explain things everyone will think we're crazy."

"They won't be far wrong." Simon looked at the sky and shrugged. All his doubts had returned.

They cast around for footprints and there were none in the fresh snow, but Sophie's mother had not shaken off the nightmare of being captured. "What if those men really do come back?" she said.

"That's the idea of the party, Lucy," Toby reassured her. "There'll be other people around, a house full of them, and that might put them right off. And I won't let you out of my sight."

"And anyway," said Sophie, "we are safe at the moment. They wouldn't risk coming back in daylight."

"If only we had the old timetable," said Jack, "that would be a help." But there was no sense in dwelling on that; there was too much to do.

They entered the station building with great caution. Nothing had changed. The parcels room seemed to store all the cold of winter, and its single window was so crusted with frozen snow that the stack of goods in the centre of the floor was shadowed and sinister. They half expected it to vanish as they approached, but the brown paper of the parcels was real, as were the sealing wax and string, and the careful penmanship of the address labels did not fade as the packages were carried into the open air.

There turned out to be more than one hamper, and the largest took three of them to lift into the truck. The name of the store they came from was stencilled on the wickerwork, and Toby was able to say, "Food ... and all in cold storage."

The corded boxes were more mysterious. Some were not heavy and were marked fragile, some rattled slightly, and in one there was a sudden whirring sound as if wheels were spinning. Toby put it to his ear and listened, and a wide grin spread across his cheeks.

"Clockwork train," he said, "must be an antique."

There was not much room in the pick-up when everything was loaded, and Simon paused before he climbed into the back with Jack. "Shouldn't one of us stay to keep watch in case the train comes back?" he asked.

"No need," said Toby cheerfully. "I've found a cosy observation spot." But he would not tell them immediately.

KEEPING WATCH

They began unloading the truck as the first snowflakes of Christmas Day floated down. "Closing in fast," said Jack. "Can't even see the hills."

"No chance of supplies from the sky." Toby Heron eased a hamper from the back of the truck. He grinned. "We should worry."

Jack's mind was on the two men. "How will we know when they get here?" he asked. Toby had said something about a place where they could keep watch.

"Grandfather Silas was very fond of the stars," was the only reply Toby gave as he helped Jack lug a hamper through the hall and along the corridor to the kitchen. Sophie and Lucy had already begun unpacking, and there were dishes and jars everywhere.

Lucy brushed hair from her brow. "There's enough food here to feed an army," she said, "but how on earth are we going to cook it all?"

Toby did not care. "Drop everything and come with me," he said.

They climbed three staircases. "We're under the tiles now," he told them and unlatched a small door. He stood aside to let them go ahead.

There was a plain staircase, narrow and steep, and it was lit by light from the sky. It seemed to go straight up into the open air, and when they climbed it they were above the roof in a small circular room with windows all around.

Lucy was thrilled. "It's a belvedere!" she said. It rested on the snow of the roof like a cabin in space.

"It's his observatory," said Toby. "Grandfather Silas watched the stars from here."

On a pedestal in the middle of the floor was a large brass telescope, and Simon was already swinging it towards the village. "There's a bit of dust on the lens," he muttered, "but I can see it."

Beyond the church tower and the rooftops, the station came into focus sharp and clear.

"We'll take turn and turn about." Toby had it all worked out. "One of us is on watch up here all day, and when it gets dark we'll keep our ears open and all doors and windows locked. But we have a lot to do before then.

161

Simon takes the first hour, everyone else downstairs."

There had never been a Christmas Day like it. Sophie and her mother, as promised, went with Jack to Forge Cottage, where Mrs Smith had begun to prepare Christmas dinner, but when she heard of all the preparations that had to be made for the feast at Heron Hall, the first thing she said was, "How on earth is that poor man going to manage all on his own?" The two women looked at each other, and with hardly a word said they packed away all the food, Jack's father brought round the car and they all went up to help at Heron Hall. "I can't help but be curious," said Mrs Smith. "He can't possibly have enough for everyone."

But there was a surprise in store for her, and for Mr Smith. Toby had not been idle. For him the party had already begun, and when they arrived he was at the top of a ladder in the entrance hall fixing candles to a Christmas tree. "Look," he said, holding one out for them to see, "the genuine thing – real candles and candle holders, a hundred years old at least."

Jack's father looked at the tin candle holder with his blacksmith's eye. "Looks like it was made yesterday," he said. "How did you come by it?"

Toby opened his mouth to reply but Mrs Smith didn't let him get a word out. "Typical men," she said, "all this work to be done, folks expecting to be fed, and all they can do is talk about candlesticks!"

"Looks like it's just out of a bran tub," said Mr Smith.

Jack was embarrassed. His father would say something as old-fashioned as that, but Toby Heron was pleased. "You can say that again. Half of this stuff came packed in bran ... or straw."

"Never mind about that, Toby Heron," Mrs Smith scolded. "Just you show me what you've done in the kitchen."

Jack put his shoulders up to his ears. She was bossing Toby just as she did him, but Toby meekly hurried to help her take off her coat. "What a relief to see you, Mrs Smith. There's so much stuff in there I've got a bit of a problem."

Jack's mother exchanged a look with Lucy Nelson. "Helpless as children," she said.

"You wonder when they're going to grow up," said Lucy.

"They'll wake up one fine day and find we've taken over the world."

Lucy looked at Toby. "And take your hat off; you don't need it indoors."

"Women to rule the world," he said. "Seems it's happened already."

"It *has*!" Sophie pulled a face at Jack.

"Join the club, Jack," said Toby. He glanced

at Jack's father, and they both took off their hats and bowed to the women.

And Christmas Day continued to show there had never been one like it.

"That's a whole ham!" said Mrs Smith, surprised to see it hanging from a hook in the ceiling. "And all these pots of preserves tied up with cloth covers – they're just like my grandmother used to make. And plum puddings! Where on earth did it all come from?"

Sophie and her mother looked at each other and felt guilty. "Toby told me it came from the same shops his great-great-grandfather used," said Lucy, but Sophie, hearing bumps from the corridor, escaped. Jack and Toby were moving a table from the library to the dining room where even the long dining table would not be big enough for all the people who were coming.

"The whole village," said Jack. News had run from house to house like wildfire.

"Keep going." Toby heaved at the table. "It'll be dark soon."

It was mid-afternoon, but clouds sagging with snow were closing in on the valley like heavy curtains. Alone in the belvedere, Sophie stamped her feet to keep warm. The cold eyepiece of the telescope against her cheek made her shudder, but as the light failed she had to keep a closer watch on the station. Twice the snow caught up in gusts of wind had fooled her into thinking that a train was steaming out of the cutting, and soon it would be too dark to spot anything.

She stretched and yawned. It was lonely up here, where old Silas had spent many a night. Perhaps he still climbed to the belvedere to watch the stars. Not a sound reached her from below, but in her mind there were hollow footsteps on the stairs, and when the single street light of the village winked like a tiny candle it so startled her that her shoulder jerked the telescope to one side. She struggled to focus it again, but now she was gazing directly at the church tower through the icy eyepiece.

The tower was where Jack had seen the Starveling Boy. She held her breath. She was on a tower herself. Suppose the Boy should wave to her … two ghosts gazing at each other over the bleak, empty fields. She forced herself to smile, but her chuckle became a trembling moan. Something moved at the tower's top.

In the church belfry the sound of a car labouring through the drifts could be heard from the road below. "Haven't heard a thing since this morning," said Reg Boston. "I want to see what's happening."

"It's not yet dark." Cousin Will was huddled in a corner where the draughts were less severe. "You'll be spotted."

"Dark enough." Boston was at the foot of

165

the spiral stair that climbed to a turret on top of the tower. The gloom in the belfry was so deep they could not see each other. "All day," he said. "I've had enough."

As he felt his way up the stair he heard the car again. He unbolted the ancient wooden door, pushed it open against the snow and kicked his way through it to the stone battlements. The car rounded the churchyard wall and snaked through the ruts towards Heron Hall just as the white wind whipped his face and blinded him. He swore and turned away.

The blizzard curtained the tower but Sophie gripped the telescope with both hands and forced herself not to run. The snow curtain danced away across the fields and the tower was bare. The Boy was only in her imagination, and Jack was calling her from below.

"Toby says it's too dark to see anything," he said. "It's time to come down."

Cousin Will stamped his feet among the pigeon droppings. "Getting darker," he said. "It will soon be time to go."

Jack's father levered the top from another packing case and stood back, shaking his head. "They used to decorate the village hall with streamers like this when I was a boy, but I ain't seen none since." He and Toby opened out a Christmas streamer that stretched from end to end of the dining room like a fat concertina. And there were paper lanterns, and fans, and dull cardboard boxes that spilled out more glittering glass trinkets than the tree could hold.

"And all brand-new!" Jack's father kept repeating. "How did you manage it, Toby?"

"Ah," said Toby mysteriously, and they stood together looking down the length of the dining room that had become a long cave of many colours.

The church door creaked open and was carefully closed as the two men stepped out. "We were lucky to find it unlocked." The coat collar buttoned over his mouth took some of the harshness out of Cousin Will's voice.

"That's because it's Christmas." Boston's dark eyebrows were already white.

"And we shall soon be rewarded, Reg, never fear."

Jack's father eased the car down the drive of Heron Hall and turned into the road. Already the windscreen was white except for the arcs made by the wipers, and his headlights were caked and the beam did not reach far in the feathery air. "Like driving through a pillow fight," he muttered. "Good job Lott's Bend ain't a very big place."

He calculated it would take at least six or seven trips to get everyone to the Hall now that he'd started, but he did wonder about how much space old Stephen Haywood with his two walking sticks would need. "He don't bend too easy," he muttered to himself. "Reckon I'd best take him first. Whoops!" He stabbed his brakes and the car slewed broadside. He lifted his foot and the car straightened. He tried to look sideways but the window was opaque. "I could've sworn I saw someone by the hedge." Not that he could even see the hedge, the blizzard was so thick.

He stopped and rolled the window down. There was nothing to be seen in the road. "Well, I didn't hit no one, that's a blessing."

He drove on, and from a dip in the snowbank two figures emerged and continued on their way to the Hall, heads down.

Heron Hall had become quiet except for the kitchen. Three fat turkeys were in the big old oven, two enormous plum puddings were boiling on the stove, trays of mince pies were waiting to be warmed, a ham was ready to be cut, and the air was filled with warm scents and a hissing and a bubbling like some great engine getting up its strength ready to move.

It was time to take a breather. Toby Heron went to Mrs Smith. "Apron off," he said. "I'm going to take you to the dining room, where you will sit down while we bring you a cup of tea."

She protested but he led her out, and the others, except for Jack's father, who was collecting the guests, heard her exclaim when, for the first time, she saw the room in all its Christmas splendour.

Toby returned to the kitchen. It was the first time the five of them had been able to talk. "Quick," he said. "We've got to make our rounds. All doors and windows to be locked before the village arrives. We know my cousin and his friend will be out there somewhere after dark, but we are certain they are not here yet. So let's make sure they will never get in." He led the way. "Upstairs windows first."

Outside, Cousin Will stood at the edge of the kitchen window. He had heard and seen enough. He signalled to Boston, who took out the key that Toby had given him long ago and unlocked a small door at the back of the house. Together, they stepped inside, silently brushing the telltale snow away from the doormat.

They made their way towards the entrance hall. The corridor was dim and they were as silent as ghosts as they trod carefully past the kitchen. The door of the dining room stood ajar. They glanced in and saw Jack's mother dozing in her chair. Ten more paces took them to the door of the library.

Toby came to the back door and shot the bolt. "Reg had a key to this door," he said, "but it's useless to him now." He looked around. "And tonight there will be plenty of people to give the alarm if a window is broken."

"What do we do if we see them?" Sophie did not want to think of coming across Reg Boston.

"Shout, and we all come running." Toby smiled. He was still enjoying himself. "But don't worry, all we have to do is to keep them out until after midnight. After that the Midwinter Watch has no power left."

Suddenly he stopped talking and held up a hand for silence. In the corridor the library door had creaked.

"What is it?" said Jack.

"Your father can't be back already, can he? I thought I heard him come in." He looked into the corridor. "Empty," he said and laughed. "I'm hearing things."

THE FEAST

It was the strangest Christmas feast anyone had ever known. It was also the best … in spite of the snow which had prevented supplies getting through to Lott's Bend.

Early in the day Sophie had called on Mrs Grist to ask her to Heron Hall and she had replied, "Bring your own food, I suppose. That Toby Heron hasn't got two pennies to rub together."

"There's plenty for everyone," said Sophie. "I've seen it."

"Well, it ain't been honestly come by, that I guarantee."

"His great-great-grandfather helped him."

"Don't be cheeky, Miss." But she agreed to come, and brought some buns and a jelly.

"Now those are just the things we are short of," Lucy Nelson told her.

"That's what I thought," said Mrs Grist.

"There's no way we're going to have a proper tuck-in, after what's been going on." She hung her coat over one of the few chairs that remained in the library which had been emptied of most of its furniture. "This don't look all that merry," she said. "I got more chairs than this in me own front room."

Sophie led her across the hall towards the dining room. There was a clatter from the kitchen, and she stopped and sniffed the air. "Somethin' cooking," she said. "What is it, bread and pull-it?"

"What's that?"

"Don't you know nothing, girl? It's what we had when we was kids – just bread, and pull it to make it go further."

Sophie opened the dining room door. Mrs Grist took one pace inside and stopped. She had a tight mouth in her stern old face, and for a moment her lips were clamped even firmer, but then the firelight at the far end of the room reached towards her, glinting on the corners of the dark old furniture, sparkling with silver on the knives and forks, dancing on the glasses all along the length of the long table and throwing strange shadows on the ceiling from the plump streamers that hung like red and green and purple sunsets among the holly. "Oh," she said, and her mouth remained open and her eyes opened wider, and for a moment or two Sophie saw Mrs Grist as she once was.

"I seen a pantomime once," she said, "when I was little and I couldn't make head or tale of it, but I knew it was lovely. This is just like it." She continued to look. "Can you believe it?"

Jack poured her a sherry and spilt some of it on her fingers. She didn't take her handkerchief to wipe them; she licked them instead and spoke confidentially to Sophie. "Boys ain't up to much," she said. "Pity we've got to have them around." Jack still stood awkwardly holding the decanter, and she held out her half-empty glass. "Right to the top this time," she said and lifted it to her lips. "Merry Christmas, young man."

Each new group, as soon as they were delivered by Jack's father, were swept inside, and the fireside seemed to expand to take them all. The dinner was going to be very late in starting but no one seemed to notice. The very youngest crawled under the table to listen to what the grown-ups were saying, or they gazed at parcels piled under the tree and tried to make out what could be inside. No one had ever seen a Christmas like this before.

Even the Christmas cards that everyone had been given with the invitation were different. The edges were shaped and embossed with leaves and flowers, and the verses inside were held in place by coloured string. "These were old-fashioned even when I was a kid," said Mr Bullock, lifting his glasses to his forehead and bringing the card close to his nose. "Where did they come from, Toby?"

"They've been lying around for quite a while," Toby told him. "I thought it was time to use them."

Mr Bullock had a collector's eye. "I wonder you can bear to hand 'em out like this. You could make a fortune if you sold 'em."

Toby's only reply was to grin and fill Mr Bullock's glass. And that became his answer to all questions, because everyone in the room found something difficult to believe. But the mystery was like every person's favourite dream, a warm tunnel in the night where they drifted from one surprise to another.

There were smiles when one turkey was brought into the room, laughter when the second entered, and cheers when Mrs Smith trooped in with the third. And there was a great handing round of dishes until every plate was full, and even those who swore they had no appetite at all had their knives and forks poised – but had to pause for crackers to snap and spill out bracelets, Chinese puzzles, pan pipes, tiny paper dresses for dolls, fans and scarf pins, and little wooden barrels with nothing in them but looking as if they could be put to use.

It was easy for those with other things on their minds to slip into the background unseen. In the hall Toby closed the door on the laughter and the clatter of dishes. "We've made the rounds," he said. "All is secure."

Lucy stood at his side. "We've even opened the doors and looked for footprints." She turned her head to Toby. "There's nothing there, is there?"

Toby shook his head and said something. Sophie saw his lips moving but did not hear his words. Her eyes were on her mother. Toby Heron was taller than Lucy Nelson, and she had to tilt her head to speak to him. It was no more than that, but Sophie's eyes misted suddenly. Her father had been tall; at least as tall as Toby Heron, and she had seen the same tilt to her mother's head when he was alive. He should have been standing beside her mother, not Toby.

"The light's gone dim." It was Simon's voice. But Sophie knew he was wrong; it was her eyes that had dimmed the hall.

"Power cut," said Jack, and Sophie blinked. The hall was truly dim, and her mother and Toby Heron had gone. A sudden draught of cold air made her turn around. The front door stood ajar and snowflakes were sweeping in. They all three ran to close it, but before they got there it swung wide and outside, in the blizzard, someone stood waiting for them.

The wind made snowflakes sting their eyes but they saw clearly enough the rags of the Starveling Boy pressed to his thin frame by the wind. He stood beside a tree, and he did not have to beckon for them to know they had to go to him. They stepped outside, and the door, caught in an eddy of the wind, slammed shut at their backs. The Boy moved away to one side and they turned to follow. Sophie alone hesitated. As the Boy moved she saw, behind him, another shape, taller, standing alone in the storm. As she watched, he raised an arm and she recognized him. She began to walk towards him, but her father's shape waved to her once more, then turned away and faded into the hurrying whiteness of the wind.

Jack came up to her. "He's gone," she said.

"I know." He put out a hand and began to lead her away.

"Did you see?" she asked. "He was with the Boy."

But Jack had seen only the Boy.

Simon joined them. "There wasn't anything there," he said. "It's only the snow. Let's get back into the warm."

Jack was looking at the front of the house. "It's not quite the same," he said. For one thing, the light inside was subdued, and the ivy that clung to the walls seemed to shake itself even when there was a lull in the wind. It was like a great dog shedding its weight of snow.

Simon himself felt doubtful, and he led the way to one of the library windows. "At least we can take a look," he said.

The drifts that lay against the wall sloped as high as the window ledges and he had to part the snow with his hands in order to get close enough to peer inside. The lights were getting even dimmer and they gazed into the large room, where the darkness was pressing in on all sides. The library was empty.

"Everyone's in the dining room," said Simon.

His hand was buried in snow on the sill, and he had been about to free it and beat it to get it warm when the silence of the other two made him glance at them. They had drawn back from the glass as if something alarmed them. He turned back to the window to see that the bookcase alongside the fireplace was swinging outwards, and he realized with a sickening hollowness what had happened. While they had looked for danger breaking in from outside, it had been with them inside the house all the time, coiled like a snake in a dark corner.

The bookcase opened and they saw Cousin Will and Reg Boston standing just within the entrance of the secret room. They did not venture into the library. They stood still, listening. Even from outside in the snow laughter could be heard from the dining room as the high point of the feast drew near. The two men knew they would not be disturbed.

Everything had gone wrong. Outside the

house Sophie, Jack and Simon stood in the snow and watched Cousin Will draw the Midwinter Watch from inside his coat. It covered the palm of his hand, too large for his fingers to completely close over it. Jack could sense the weight of it as it had lain in his own hand, and all that Cousin Will had to do to bring back the past was to press the stud that opened it. Jack raised his hand to punch a hole in the window but he was too late. The stud was pressed and the watchcase flew open.

And then nothing. They stood in the snow gazing into the library, and Simon took a pace back as if he wanted no more to do with it. "I thought so," he mumbled. "It didn't do a thing."

Sophie had not moved from the window. "They are very still," she whispered.

The men were motionless, holding themselves tense. They also were waiting for something to happen.

Simon turned his head away and listened. There was, after all, something odd about the night that made him lower his voice. "The whole house has gone quiet," he murmured.

No sound reached them from the crowded dining room. It was as silent as if it was empty, and they all three turned back to the window. The men remained as they were and all was so uncannily still that Sophie's eyes wandered the room seeking for any sign of movement. It was lit by candles. She did not remember having seen candles there. The flames were perfect little almonds balancing on the candle tips without a flicker in the still air. Not a single tremor, even though...

She pulled back her head so sharply that the others turned to her. She risked pointing, putting her finger so close to the glass that anyone within the room could have seen her. "There," she said, "look at that candle by the fireplace."

The candlestick stood on a table close enough to the fireplace for its flame to be caught in the draught of chimney and to be bent towards the fire. The flame was leaning far over, but was motionless. Even a wisp of smoke from its tip streaked the air but was quite still.

"It's a trick of the light," said Simon. "It'll change."

But the smoke hung where it was, and the men remained as they were.

Somewhere from among the trees an owl's hollow cry shivered in the night, and they stepped back. The silent house looked down on them and seemed to be listening as their feet crunched through the snow's crust towards the front door. They stood on the step and pushed it open.

The hall was as they had left it, but within the dark corridor that led to the kitchen there was a light. It was blue and seemed uncertain, casting patchy shadows over the face and dress of the woman who, for a long moment, seemed to be coming towards them. But she did not move, and the dish she was carrying with a round pudding in its nest of brandy flames did not even tremble. The flames stood in blue peaks and some had separated from the rest and had flicked up into the air, where they hung in space and shed a ghostly glare on the face which they had not recognized. Jack's mother was smiling, but her face was as fixed as the rags of blue flame suspended in front of her.

Sophie saw Jack pause, bewildered, but she drew him towards the library. That was where they had to go. She turned the handle wondering if it, too, was rigid and would not stir, but it moved and the door swung smoothly open and they went in.

She saw the two men hunched over as they gazed down at the Midwinter Watch, and she allowed the door handle to rattle as she released it. They did not look up.

She was sure of nothing. Perhaps she was in a dream. "Jack," she whispered, "can you hear me?"

"Yes." He could hear her but he, too, had to test what was happening. He reached towards a candle flame and touched it. There was a sensation of warmth in his fingertips and he rubbed them together within the flame but could feel nothing more than a slipperiness that slid like silk. When he took his hand away the oval of the flame had not changed.

Simon went ahead and stood directly in front of the men. Neither of them moved, and his doubts were a thing of the past. "It's obvious what's happened," he said. "They made a mistake. They've stopped everything in the house – including themselves."

The two men had been cautious. They had pushed the shelves open but had not stepped out into the library. They stood just within the entrance of the secret room and gazed down at the Midwinter Watch. Their lips were slightly parted, and firelight glinted in the corner of Cousin Will's eye. But he did not blink and the glint did not move. The men had the ghastliness of perfect waxworks, and Sophie's first thought was to push them over, but Simon was reaching for the Watch.

"No!" Jack prevented him.

"Why not? It's what we want."

"We've got to see where they went wrong." Jack bent closer. A strand of black hair which had fallen across Boston's face swayed slightly. Jack almost jumped back, but clenched his jaw and held himself still. The lines of Cousin Will's face had frozen into a tight smile that seemed to taunt him, daring him to act, but he dragged his own eyes away to look down at

181

the face of the Midwinter Watch.

Cousin Will's finger was still on the stud and the cover had sprung open. It had started to bring back the past; the candles proved that. Then everything had stopped.

Simon also bent close. "Can you see what's gone wrong?"

The silence in the room was intense. Jack shook his head. He had to fight to hold back his panic. "I don't know!" The sound of his own voice startled him and he drew back, but not a muscle twitched the waxwork faces and the house had not come to life. The silence was so deep that Sophie realized there was not even the tick of a clock. Her eyes came back to rest on the two men. There was no sound of any sort ... but surely there was one particular sound that was absolutely vital.

Suddenly she stepped between the two boys, and for the first time looked closely at the Mid-winter Watch. She tilted her head to listen, and knew the sound she did not hear. The Watch was not ticking. She bent closer. There was a second hand. It was motionless.

She glanced swiftly at the boys and neither tried to prevent her as she reached for the Watch. She had to touch Cousin Will's fingers. They were not glossy waxworks. Not cold. Cousin Will's fingers were warm, and flexible. She had to bend them with her own shrinking fingers as she eased the golden egg from his grip. She was gasping as she stood looking at it. Nothing had changed.

"Try it," said Jack. "Press the button again."

She did so. Nothing happened. "It's stopped," she told them. "It's broken." And it slowly dawned on them that they were trapped in an endless nightmare. Nothing in the house would ever move again.

Jack took the Watch. How could it be broken when it had kept going for a hundred years? It had not been touched or even seen for all that time and had not stopped once. Not once. The words echoed in his brain. Not once. Like the old grandfather clock. That had never stopped, and the Watch had swung in its pendulum for a hundred years without stopping, but now, only a day after it had been taken out... And then he knew.

"It's not been wound up!" he said. "It has run down!"

There was no winder. Jack turned the Watch in his hands. There was nothing to turn the spring. But the pendulum had managed to do it. There was a connection. He remembered how he had fumbled the Watch free from the spindle inside the pendulum rod. He looked down at it; there was a small hole in the watch-case where the spindle had fitted and turned like a key as the pendulum swung to wind the watchspring. "That's the keyhole," he murmured. "All we need is something to reach inside and wind it up." He looked around. There was nothing.

"Would that do?" Sophie was pointing at Cousin Will. She touched his spectacles. "The side piece is thin."

Jack lifted the glasses from Cousin Will's nose, prised out one of the lenses, put his thumb through the hole and wrenched off the metal side piece. It was satisfying. "I'm sorry about that," he said to the stiff face, and let the glasses fall to the floor.

The thin metal slid easily into the socket of the Watch, but just as Jack was about to turn it Simon became cautious. "Not in here," he said. "We don't know what might happen."

They swung the shelves back into place, leaving the men shut in the dark, before they left the silent house and stood again at the library window.

"Now," said Jack, and slowly began to turn the key. He felt the ratchet within the Watch click once, and in the moonlight he saw the second hand flick into life. Then he looked no more.

The library glowed with more light, and the room itself was different. The furniture had changed and on the other side of the room an old man was working at a desk. They were watching Toby Heron's great-great-grand-father. He had his back towards them and the

184

light from a shaded lamp shone on his bald head, and also glinted on what lay on the desk. Grandfather Silas was doing his accounts. Little stacks of small gold coins stood in front of him, row upon row of them, and with the tip of his pen he was counting them. He was completing his task, for he made a note on a sheet of paper, stretched himself, yawned, and left the library.

A man carrying a tray entered the room and put it down on a table next to the desk. It was Grandfather Silas's supper, and his man-servant gazed down at the ranks of gold coins before he reluctantly turned away to make up the fire with new logs and plump the cushions in the fireside chairs, but his eyes were continually turning towards the desk and its glinting guineas. He bit his lip as if he was turning over important matters in his mind as he went towards the door. He was turning the handle when he paused, thought for a moment longer, then made a decision.

He peered into the corridor, shut the door, and acted swiftly. He took a large red hand-kerchief from his pocket, spread it on the desk, heaped all the gold coins on to it and was knotting the ends with trembling fingers when some sound from beyond the door alarmed him. He made a frantic effort to stuff the bundle inside his shirt, but the bulge gave him away, and in a panic he went to the fireplace, dropped the bundle behind the log basket and ran to the door calling out, "Yes, sir, I'll be with you at once!"

They had seen the theft and knew where the gold was hidden. "Now's our chance!" Jack straightened. All they had to do was run inside and grab the bundle.

They were still stepping back when a sound made them pause. The window to their right was hidden by ivy, but they heard a creak as the window was pulled open and a shape climbed inside. The touch of snowflakes made their skin crawl. Some other watcher had been alongside them, looking in. A furtive shadow crept forward. It was bent over and its head swayed from side to side, as if it was fearful of being seen. But even before it entered the ring of bright light around the desk Sophie recognized it.

The Starveling Boy was crossing the room. And he was no ghost. Sophie heard the rags that bound his feet scrape the floor and saw the patches of wetness and snow he left behind. It was the food that drew him.

Everything he possessed was in a sack slung over his shoulder. There was a pie on a plate. He scooped it into the sack. A cake joined it, and it was only then that he made for the fireplace.

He was limping on his frozen feet, and his face was pinched and blue with cold, and at

186

first he seemed only to be warming himself at the fire despite the risk. But then he stooped to the log basket. "Oh no," Sophie moaned, and she found herself pleading with him not to do it as he lifted up the weighty bundle of coins. He glanced towards the open window, but when he moved it was only to turn his back on it.

She pressed her knuckles to her mouth, but the words came out. "He's going to the desk!" she murmured. "He's putting the money back!"

Outside the window none of them breathed. The Boy took three shuffling paces, then stopped. He was listening. They heard nothing, but the Boy suddenly spun around and headed away from the door. He had reached the fireplace when the door opened and the manservant stood there. The man was full of guilt and overflowing with caution, and for a long moment he was too afraid to react to what he saw. And the Starveling Boy was gripped in a panic that made all his actions jerky and stupid. He turned to the fireplace as if to hide what he was doing, and he appeared to be struggling with his sack as if he was trying, but failing, to stuff the money into it. They watched in agony as he stooped alongside the mantel while the manservant was already running towards him.

Sophie opened her mouth to shout a warning and she heard Jack mutter, "Come on! Come on!" between his teeth, when all the candles in the room dimmed suddenly, the running man seemed to pause in mid step and the Boy, who had begun to turn, stood rigidly. The candles flared and dimmed, and flared again, and at each flash of brightness the man and boy moved flickeringly forward like figures slowed by water.

"The Watch!" The cry came from Simon. "It's slowing down!"

Jack raised it close to his face. The second hand laboured from tick to tick as the Watch ran down. He had been too cautious. He reached to wind it, but the improvised key had fallen into the snow and was lost. He shook it.

The Boy gained the window and the man roared, "Stop thief!" just as laughter rose up from the dining room, and within the library the shelves once more swung open and Cousin Will and Reg Boston reappeared.

They saw the Boy leap from the window just as the Watch stopped and the charging man-servant vanished. The past had vanished, and they were again in the present time. Yet, outside the house, they still saw the Boy. He made no footprints as he landed in the snow but his ragged shape continued to run and they followed. He disappeared round the corner of the house, and they caught sight of him again as he crossed the stableyard. Ahead of him was an outbuilding almost obscured by a drift of snow piled halfway to its roof, but the Boy made no attempt to avoid it. He flung himself at its feet and began to crawl inside it. Within a second he was gone and they were faced with a smooth sweep of snow that had never been disturbed.

"What's in there?" Jack pointed at the building as he turned to Sophie.

"It's falling down." That was all she knew. "It's empty."

"It was his hiding place." Jack was sure of it. "He crawled somewhere."

Simon had found the entrance. The door was hanging crooked on its hinges, and his torch was probing the shadows inside.

"It's dangerous in there," said Sophie, but they went in together.

Simon pointed his beam at the wall which held back the snowdrift outside. "There's nothing here," he said, but Jack went ahead. A floorboard cracked beneath him.

"It's all rotten!" Sophie's warning was too late. A board bent beneath Jack's foot and collapsed. He fell forward and another worm-riddled board fell in. He stood up to his knees in the cavity under the floor. Simon shone the torch to help him out, and Jack was clutching Sophie's hand when they all three saw the same thing. A heap of rags lay on the earth beneath the boards.

Jack heaved himself free and they stood gazing down into the Starveling Boy's grave. He had run from the house to his hiding place, and in that winter long ago he had died. His pitiful bones lay there covered by the rags that had not been sufficient to protect him from the cold, and to one side lay the sack that contained all his belongings. And a fortune in gold.

They stood where they were. They could not disturb the Starveling Boy's resting place. Now was not the time.

"Let's go and tell Toby Heron," said Jack quietly, and a voice from behind his back answered him just as softly.

"You may if you wish," it said, and the breath of the speaker was so close he felt it on his neck. His hair bristled and he spun around to see the glint of Cousin Will's smile before the weight of Reg Boston's arm sent him flying.

Boston's bulk charged the other two down, the torch rolled on the floor and its light fell on Cousin Will stooping to the gap and coming up with the sack in his hand. The torch was kicked into the darkness, the door was heaved shut, and by the time they battered it open, the gears of the pick-up truck were whining as it accelerated, slammed into a gatepost and rocked away down the drive.

They yelled uselessly after it, but the two men were gone, and with them went Toby Heron's treasure.

MISTLETOE

Sophie shivered. Jack did not know whether he was allowed to put his arm around her; if she had been only slightly less pretty he would have felt safe enough to do so. Instead he said, "Did they hurt you?"

Her jaw was clamped too tight for her to speak. She shook her head. Why wouldn't he touch her?

"We'll chase them." There were other cars in the drive. He began to move towards the house but she held his sleeve.

"Listen," she said.

From far away, like a screech of victory, the whistle of a train taunted them across the snow.

"They're gone." Simon manufactured a shrug. "We'll never see them again."

They stood together, three dark figures in the endless white of the landscape, and after a moment began to move slowly towards the house. They had yet to tell Toby Heron of their failure.

Sophie still fought to stop herself trembling. "Under the floorboards," she said to Jack, "are you sure it was the Boy?"

He had been closest. He had seen grey finger bones. "His hand touched the sack," he said.

The cold stung Sophie's eyes and she allowed tears to wet her cheeks. "He had to steal the food," she said, "he was hungry." The money was another matter; she did not think of it.

Jack was cold. His mind was filled with the Starveling Boy creeping under the floorboards to die in the dark. Someone … all of them … would give the Boy a proper burial. He tried to think of that.

"I wish we could see him again," said Sophie. Once would be enough, now that she knew what had become of him. The Mid-winter Watch was in Jack's pocket, but its power had gone. It would never carry them back to see the Boy alive. Ahead of them the glow from the dining room window coloured the snow, but the Starveling Boy remained in the cold and dark.

The library was in darkness as they trudged past. Simon noted that a window was still open and the snow beneath it was disturbed where the two men had climbed out. But that was also in the past; it no longer mattered. His eyes idly moved to the next window, and he stopped short.

"What is it?" Jack was alongside him. Simon pointed. Not everyone was at the feast. Someone was moving in the library. They watched as a pale face came near to the glass and gazed down on them.

"Is it him?" Sophie could not be sure. The night air had frosted the window pane, and the face was indistinct. But then a thin hand was raised and a finger moved against the glass. It did not beckon, but it seemed to be making a sign.

"It's writing!" said Simon.

They could see letters forming in the frost, but there was not enough light to make them clear. Simon shone his torch. The letters, written from inside, were the wrong way round, and the instant the beam fell on the glass the writing finger ceased and the face vanished.

They ran through the hall, flung open the library door and switched on the lights. The room was empty, and whoever had written in the frost on the window pane had had a shaky and uncertain hand. "And he can't spell," said Simon. He read out what was written: "Chimbley!" He was still laughing as Sophie took the torch from his hand and went with Jack to the fireplace.

The fire had burned low in the wide grate.

She crouched and shone the torch into the black throat of the chimney as Jack reached up behind the mantel. There was a shelf in the brickwork. He felt along it. The soot was fluffy and warm but soon his fingers touched an obstruction. He tugged. It came free but he was unable to hold it and a black, sooty bundle fell into the hearth and split open. They looked down, and what they saw showed them that the Starveling Boy was no thief.

"That's what he wanted us to know." Sophie looked wildly around the room, but the only trace of the Boy was the writing that was already fading on the window. "He hid it." A pile of gold pieces lay among the soot in the hearth.

Simon nodded. "So that's why he hung about near the fireplace when he should have made a run for it."

"He wanted to stay," said Sophie, "but he had to run because that man called him a thief. He meant to come back and tell Grandfather Silas, but..." Her voice trailed away.

"He never had a chance," Jack finished for her. "The night was too cold for him."

A thought occurred to Simon. "So what do you reckon was in the sack?" he said.

"Stale pie," said Jack.

The train whistle must have shrieked just as Cousin Will and Reg Boston had spilled the contents of the sack into their laps.

"Crumbs!" cried Simon. "What a surprise!" and they were still laughing as they crossed the hall to the dining room.

They opened the door to a great cheer, but it wasn't for them. It was for the provider of the feast, Toby Heron, who stood at the top of the table. Sophie's mother was alongside him, and Jack's father, more red-faced than ever from eating and drinking, came up behind them with a sprig of mistletoe. Jack winced, but someone shouted, "Now's the time, Toby!" And when he did kiss Lucy Nelson it lasted so long that Sophie wanted to say she was disgusted, but then she looked sideways at Jack, and they both blushed and said nothing.

JET SMOKE AND DRAGON FIRE
by Charles Ashton

"The dragon roared, and roared again; and mingling with the smoke left by the aeroplane, the dragon's flame went spinning and coiling."

The odd thing about Sparrow's village is that although it has all the gadgets of the modern world – telephones, televisions, calculators – no one knows how they work. But this mystery is nothing to the extraordinary events that transform the lives of Sparrow and his friends after an encounter with the magical Puckel and, of course, with the dragon itself...

"A superb writer... Sensationally good."
The Sunday Telegraph

"A racy story full of fantastic adventures."
Junior Education

LONE WOLF
by Kristine L. Franklin

Three years ago, following a family tragedy, Perry and his dad left the city and moved to a remote cabin in the woods. Perry spends much of his time with his dog, Rhonda, in the cave that's his secret hideout. Then goofy, inquisitive Willow Pestalozzi and her large family move into the empty house nearby and Perry finds himself having to face things he's tried so hard to forget...

Kristine L. Franklin's tender, moving story reveals how learning to laugh again also means being able, at last, to cry.

FIRE, BED AND BONE
by Henrietta Branford

England's peasants are tired of the hardship and injustice they suffer at the hands of harsh landlords. Rebellion is in the air, bringing dramatic and violent upheaval to the lives of families like Rufus, Comfort and their children – and even to dogs, like the old hunting bitch, who is the narrator of this unforgettable tale.

This gripping and vivid story by a Smarties Book Prize-winning author is an extraordinary achievement, depicting the tumult and tragedy of the Peasants' Revolt through the eyes, ears and nose of a dog.

DOUBLE VISION
by Diana Hendry

"People would do a lot better if they could see double like me... I mean seeing things two ways – with the head and the heart."

Growing up in a small, North West coastal town in the 1950s, fifteen-year-old Eliza Bishop finds life unbearably claustrophobic. But to her small, fearful sister Lily, the seaside setting affords unlimited scope for her imagination. Through these two very different pairs of eyes a memorable range of characters, events and emotions is brought clearly into vision.

"Succeeds totally where very few books do, as a novel which bestrides the two worlds of adult and children's fiction with total success in both... The stuff of which the very best fiction is wrought." *The Sunday Times*

THE BEAST OF WHIXALL MOSS
by Pauline Fisk

So what if he can never satisfy his mother's desire for perfection and his brother can? So what if he's lonely out on Whixall Moss? He doesn't care – or so he likes to tell himself. Then one day he sees, in a boat hidden on the creek, a beautiful, fabulous beast. At once he is filled with a wild longing: he must own it. But the boat's mysterious inhabitants have other ideas...

Gripping and powerful, this novel by Smartie's Book Prize Winner Pauline Fisk is a tale that will live long in the imagination.

THE FLOWER KING
by Lesley Howarth

The narrator of this story doesn't just see colours, he *feels* them. At home, the colour is mainly panic-button red. But on Saturdays, visiting old Mrs Pinder, a hopeful yellow floods in. It's the yellow of the daffodil fields where "Pinny" worked as a child for William Bowhays Johns, the Flower King, whose tragic story lies at the heart of this absorbing tale.

"Characterisation is deft, the descriptive passages lyrical, the dialogue tone perfect."
Michael Morpurgo, The Guardian

"A pleasure … assured and original." *Gillian Cross, The Times Educational Supplement (Books of the Year)*

THE GHOST OF RAVENS CRAG
by Hugh Scott

It begins on the motorway. The Smiths – Mum and Dad, Sammy, Miff (the narrator) and baby Bertie – are on their way to the Lake District, when they pass an old man in a brown suit, standing on the verge, smiling...

Then, on the slip road, they pass him again, ... and again... On arrival at their holiday destination, *The Ravens Crag Hotel*, the Smiths soon find themselves drawn in to a dark supernatural mystery, involving a boxed-in pew at the local church, a Devil-worshipping child-murderer and the ghosts of dead children. And to be drawn in is to be in danger. Deadly danger...

"Horror and good writing don't often go hand in hand – Scott is a master of the genre." *The Sunday Telegraph*

WHATEVER HAPPENED
TO KATY-JANE?
by Jean Ure

Waking in hospital after a road accident, Katy-Jane quickly realizes that something is not right; in fact, many things are wrong. The strange mousy woman by her bedside claims to be her mum; but her mum died over a year ago.

She has different friends too, and different likes and interests – she even looks different. And yet she feels the same. How can she be Katy-Jane and not Katy-Jane? Whatever can have happened to her? And, most important of all, will she ever again be the person she once was? Jean Ure's gripping story is full of mystery and suspense.

STRAY
by A. N. Wilson

Stray is the wonderfully imagined life story of Pufftail, an alley-cat. It is a tale of adventure, love, high comedy and terrible tragedy...

"A must for moggie maniacs." *The Daily Mail*

"A clever, moving, imaginative book for cat lovers of any age." *The Daily Telegraph*

"A.N. Wilson has pulled a very distinguished cat out of his hat. It is an excellent book... A book for the whole family." *The Spectator*

THE BURNING BABY AND
OTHER GHOSTS
by John Gordon

A teenage girl disappears mysteriously a few days before bonfire night; two youths out skating see something grisly beneath the ice; an elderly spinster feeds her young charge to the eels... In these five supernatural tales, the spirits of the dead seek to exact a terrifying revenge on those who have wronged them.

"Strong meat, but never gratuitously nasty."
The Independent on Sunday

"Chilling and addictive... Outstanding." *In Brief*

"John Gordon's ability to hold the tension is as strong as ever." *Books For Keeps*

WHITE WOLF
by Henrietta Branford

To the boy, Jesse, the beautiful white wolf is Snowy, his dog-like companion; to Jesse's trader father, he's a safeguard against Indian attack; to the native people themselves he's a creature of mythological power and magic. But what the young wolf longs for more than anything is to be with his own kind, one of the pack, running, hunting, singing, out in the wild... This is his thrilling story.

"A writer of extraordinary talent... She has a sure-footedness that looks so like instinct it's easy to miss the craft." *Philip Pullman, The Guardian*

"Vividly captures the sense of an animal fighting for survival." *Michael Thorn, Literary Review*

THE ENCHANTED VILLAGE
by Enid Richemont

Something strange is happening to the village of Tremarion.

Throughout August it has been under a spell of grey, sultry weather with neither sunshine nor rain, while the rest of Cornwall has been enjoying blue skies, breezes and summer showers. Local mystic Cassandra Pugh claims that it's the sign of something supernatural, but no one ever takes her seriously. Then the fairground people arrive. Bearing the names of ancient gods and goddesses and dressed spectacularly to match, they take the village by storm. Piers is their particular favourite, having persuaded his mother to give shelter to one of them, Demetria, and has been rewarded with the gift of a gold apple. Or *is* it a gift? As events take a more sinister turn, Piers begins to fear that the gift might actually be a curse...

Enid Richemont's entertaining and suspenseful tale gives an ingenious modern-day spin to some of the most colourful characters and stories of classical mythology.

TWICE TIMES DANGER
by Enid Richemont

Have you seen this girl? Missing from home. Daisie Trevelyan. Aged eleven.

Becca and Daisie have been best friends for two years but their friendship has grown increasingly strained during the summer holidays, before starting at different schools. Then Perdita turns up: posh, bossy, rich Dita, so identical to Daisie they could be twins. And from the moment the two girls meet, Becca is an outsider, a stooge in their games of swapping identities. But what begins as a joke to fool Dita's au pair becomes deadly serious when Daisie goes missing. Who has taken her and why? Becca must solve this sinister mystery to prevent twice times danger turning into double death.

MISTER SPACEMAN
by Lesley Howarth

Thomas Moon is a space freak. His room's done up like the Mir Space Station. He hunts the websites daily for space news and stories. He wants to be an astronaut. And according to the mysterious email he's just received, addressed to Mister Spaceman, his dreams are about to come true...

"Each of her books is an invigorating display of verbal fireworks, and a fresh foray into the imgination." *Gillian Cross, TES*

PAULINA
by Lesley Howarth

"The whole room seemed to close in on me. A feeling of dread rushed out from the walls. My mouth felt dry...

Poor 'lina, the air conditioning hummed. *Poor 'lina, poor 'lina, poor 'lina...*"

When Rebecca and her family swap their little cottage in South West England for George and Annie's luxurious home in New England – complete with Buick and swimming pool – it seems as if they've got the better of the holiday deal. But that's before Paulina.

Anything you want, ask Paulina, says George. But it's what *Paulina* wants that starts to worry Rebecca. Her hideous pink plastic belt keeps appearing all over the house and garden. She delivers newspapers that are sixteen years out of date. She leaves a nasty surprise in the pool. And then Rebecca realizes: there are two Paulinas and one of them is dead. Very dead.

And boy, is she ever mad at Rebecca...

A dream holiday becomes a terrifying nightmare in this taut, spine-chilling story by the award-winning author of *MapHead*.

MAPHEAD
by Lesley Howarth

Greetings from the Subtle World –

Twelve-year-old MapHead is a visitor from the Subtle World that exists side by side with our own. Basing himself in a tomato house, the young traveller has come to meet his mortal mother for the first time. But, for all his dazzling alien powers, can MapHead master the language of the human heart?

Highly commended for the Carnegie Medal and the WH Smith Mind Boggling Books Award.

"Weird, moving and funny by turns... Lesley Howarth has a touch of genius." *Chris Powling, Books for Keeps*

"Offbeat and original... Strongly recommended to all who enjoy a good story." *Books For Your Children*

TANGO'S BABY
by Martin Waddell

Brian Tangello – Tango – is not one of life's romantic heroes. Even his few friends are amazed to learn of his love affair with young Crystal O'Leary, the girl he fancies and who seemed to have no interest in him. Next thing they know, she's pregnant – and that's when the real story of Tango's baby begins. By turns tragic and farcical, it's a story in which many claim a part, but few are able to help Tango as he strives desperately to keep his new family together.

"Stylishly written, sensitive, funny and moving… A book with a depth that can only reward all who read it." *The Times*

"Waddell is as ever an excellent storyteller." *The Independent*

"Brilliantly written." *The Sunday Telegraph*

SOMETHING RARE AND SPECIAL
by Judy Allen

A moving and enthralling story by a Whitbread Award-winning author.

Following her parents' divorce, Lyn moves out of London with her mother to a house by the sea. At first, missing her old friends and city life, Lyn feels like a fish out of water. But then, down on the sands, she meets Bill Walker, who opens her eyes to a new world – and something rare and special...

"A sensitive story, rich with thoughtful atmosphere." *Junior Education*

MONKEY
by Veronica Bennett

"Hey, Pritchard! Monkey-features! Monkey, monkey, monkey!"

By teenager Harry Pritchard's own admission, he's a dork. At school he's taunted and bullied by the vicious "Brigadier" Gerard Fox; at home he's weighed down by the chores his mother sets him – the worst of which is having to look after his irritating little sister, Emma. At least, that *was* the worst until Mum volunteers him to visit a severely disabled patient of hers, Simon Schofield, two evenings a week. She says it'll do him good. But how can being a helpless cripple's monkey help him end Brig's bullying? Or get him a part in the Drama Club play? Or win the attentions of beautiful Louise Harding, the girl of his dreams? Simon, though, turns out to be quite different from what Harry imagines and, after meeting him, Harry's life undergoes dramatic – and traumatic – changes!

Touching, perceptive and thought-provoking, Veronica Bennett's book is a first novel of outstanding assurance and quality.

BADGER ON THE BARGE
by Janni Howker

"This set of five stories, each concerned with a relationship between young and old, is quality stuff… Not to be missed." *The Times Educational Supplement*

These fine stories abound with absorbing situations and memorable characters. Meet cussed, rebellious Miss Brady, who lives with a badger on a barge; the reviled old shepherd Reicker; Sally Beck, topiary gardener with an extraordinary past; the reclusive Egg Man; proudly independent Jakey … and the young people whose lives they profoundly affect.

Winner of the International Reading Association Children's Book Award. Shortlisted for the Whitbread Children's Novel Award and the Carnegie Medal.

THE HOLLOW LAND
by Jane Gardam

"Nine stories, rich in character and incident, combine to form a mini saga of two families – one local to the Cumbrian fells, one 'incomers' from London... The writing is individual, observant, funny: a celebration of a landscape and its people." *Books For Keeps*

"Authentic gold in every syllable... A book for readers, for people – of whatever age." *Junior Bookshelf*

"A remarkable book." *The Times*

"Not to be missed." *The Guardian*

Winner of the Whitbread Children's Novel Award.

THE PECULIAR POWER
OF TABITHA BROWN
by Mary Hooper

"I looked down at myself. I saw black fur. I saw paws. And I knew immediately what had happened."

Tabitha Brown is surprised to learn she's been left a cat cushion in Great-aunt Mitzi's will. But soon, the true nature of her aunt's legacy becomes clear. Landing on her feet, Tabitha realizes she has inherited a peculiar and extraordinary power – and she quickly sets about making good use of it!

Intriguing and highly enjoyable, Mary Hooper's story is guaranteed to make you purr.

SO MUCH TO TELL YOU
by John Marsden

Scarred, literally, by her past, Marina has withdrawn into silence.

She speaks to no one. But, set the task of writing a diary by her English teacher, she finds a way of expressing her thoughts and feelings and of exploring the traumatic events that have caused her distress. There is so much she has to say...

"Beautifully written... The heroine's perceptiveness, sense of humour and fairmindedness temper the tragedy and offer a splendid read." *The Times Educational Supplement*

"A moving chronicle of personal recovery." *The Observer*

THE DEVIL AND HIS BOY
by Anthony Horowitz

Heading for an exciting new life in London, Tom Falconer is ambushed by the murderous Ratsey.

Helpless and alone, the orphan gallops towards the great city, where an assortment of colourful rogues and a number of mortal dangers await him. But it's not until the first night of a new play, *The Devil and his Boy*, that Tom discovers the fate of Elizabethan England rests in his hands.

Drawing on actual people and places from the Elizabethan period, this is a vividly atmospheric, fast-paced and thrilling adventure story.

RIDING THE WAVES
by Theresa Tomlinson

"Don't let the waves frighten you. They can knock you down, but they can't stop you getting up and trying again."

When Matt goes to visit Florrie as part of a school history project, he doesn't expect to enjoy himself. Why should some cranky old lady's reminiscences interest him? He'd much rather be down on the beach with the surfers, riding the waves – if only he had a board... There's a lot more to Florrie, though, than meets the eye, and her personal history has some uncanny similarities to Matt's own!

"Sparkling, moving and funny." *The Guardian*

MORE WALKER PAPERBACKS
For You to Enjoy